The Ladies of Pagodaville
Book Two

By

Ellen Bennett

Ellen Bennett

DEDICATION

FOR

SJVS

The Ladies of Pagodaville

This is a work of fiction. All characters, locales, and events are either products of the author's imagination or are used fictitiously.

THE LADIES OF PAGODAVILLE – BOOK TWO

Copyright © 2020 by Ellen Bennett.

All rights reserved. No part of this book may be reproduced in any manner whatsoever without written permission from the publisher, save for brief quotations used in critical articles or reviews.

Photo credit:

Published by Smiling Dog Publications, LLC

www.smilingdogpublicationsllc.com

ISBN: 978-0-9980277-1-5

First Edition, September 2020

Printed in the United States of America

ACKNOWLEDGMENTS

Editor
Elizabeth Andersen

Beta Readers:
Michelle Byrd, Mari Stark, Joyce Dodrill-Krieger, Diane Long, Renae C. Feldpausch

Cover design:
Ann McMan

Author photograph:
Katherine Mumma

Format Guru:
Karen D. Badger

IN this situation of writing fiction, I surround myself with characters who may or may not do what I intend for them. When they vanish from existence for a while (like, months), I am lost. If it were not for the home-front beta listener to endure chapter after chapter of rewrites, my brain might easily short out and become a blob of gray mass. A heartfelt and well-deserved thank you to Suzanne J. VanderSalm for listening, commenting, drifting off when necessary, and applauding. You are my rock between hard places.

Your E-

So many people from your past know a version of you that doesn't exist anymore.

Tiny Buddha

PROLOGUE
Monday, September 19, 1980
Redhook Minimum Security Correctional Facility
Redhook County
Miami, Florida

Irene Boule parked her beat-up tan Camaro at the far end of the facility lot. She pulled the rearview mirror toward her face, applied more color to her lips, blotted with a scrunched-up tissue, dabbed at the corners of her mouth, and then took a deep breath.

This was going to be her finest hour.

It was ten o'clock sharp in the morning. The visitation hours for professionals—lawyers, doctors, and law enforcement officers—was between 10:00 a.m. and 2:00 p.m. Irene was going to play this by the book.

As she walked confidently toward the visitor entrance, she felt a sense of importance.

Chest out, head high!

She counted on Georgie's intel that the shift staff was different from when she normally visited. To make sure she was not recognized, she had tamed her high-teased hair into a straight flip earlier this morning, with just a hint of bangs sweeping her forehead. She even donned a headband to make herself look extra-collegiate. She thought it would be prudent to wear her glasses instead of her contact lenses. The ensemble was perfect.

Outside the entrance to the facility, Irene gave her breasts one more quick shove toward the middle of her 42 double D-cup bra, and then she undid one more button on her chartreuse-colored blouse, making it three down the line with plenty of tanned cleavage showing.

The Ladies of Pagodaville

Instead of wearing her usual silver chain heavily laden with charms around her neck, she opted for something a bit more professional—a gold necklace that she lifted from a local costume shop just last week for this occasion.

She relished the fact that she was entering a prison-like facility with stolen goods on her body. The peach-colored skirt suit she wore was a hand-me-down from a drag-queen friend who had left the store without paying for it (accidentally) a few months ago.

Irene opened the door to the facility and entered the waiting area. The guard on duty, Gary Doper, was a tall, lanky guy with leftover acne divots on his face, a thin set mouth, hooked nose, and watery brown eyes. Georgie assured Irene that Gary turned stupid in the presence of a hot woman and that it wouldn't take much to derail him.

Gary sat behind plexiglass, and he motioned for her to approach.

He visibly reddened as she employed her best vixen walk toward him.

She cooed professionally. "Good morning, officer …" She made a big deal about checking his name tag, "Dope. Uh, so sorry, *Doper*. I'm here to see inmate George DiLaRusso."

Gary scowled then nodded, "Are you on the schedule?"

"Yes, Clare O'Toole." Then after a beat, why not try it out for size? "Attorney."

Gary looked down at his list, but his eyes kept skipping back to her cleavage like a broken record. "Sure. Let me just … ah … hmm. I don't see you here on the list."

She delved into the role, cocking her head and furrowing her eyebrows. "No? My associate, Don Holland, was supposed to set this up for me. He was going to come but … his baby boy had to have surgery this morning."

Gary asked, "Hope it's nothing serious?"

Irene shook her head and, with a look of concern on her face, said, "Circumcision."

Gary paled for a moment, then licked his lips and swallowed, his Adam's apple bobbing quickly.

"Um, so you're …" He tried to look down at his list once again.

"Clare O'Toole. I work with Don. He sent me with some papers for George to sign."

"Oh yeah, Don. Yes. Well, you can leave the papers with me since ..."

"Ah, no, I really can't." She leaned in so her breasts were parked on the counter in front of the glass. Her bra was clearly exposed now, but she was on a roll. She watched Gary flinch as if she had just put her bosom in his hands. "You see, I have to explain some things to George, what with his parole coming up in three months. These are very"—she leaned in even farther—"very sensitive papers." She whispered the last line.

"Well, okay." Gary fumbled with his pen. "Spell your name." His hand was jittery. He didn't even ask her for an ID—which she had but knew was a long shot. The downtown Miami "establishment" where she went for a new ID was not exactly the cream of the crop. The clerk, a seedy-looking sort with several teeth missing named Vance, told her it was the best she was going to get in town, for the money that was.

"Of course," she purred. "C-l-a-r ..."

The rest was easy.

Gary nodded his head for her to move on, his face firehouse red.

Irene clacked her six-inch heels on the concrete floor with purpose as she strode toward the Silo. She knew Gary was watching her. She could smell his sweat.

The Silo, a windowless, brightly lit high-rise tube where visitors entered from the lobby and waited for a guard overhead to mechanically close the lobby door and open a bigger metal door for entrance to the prison yard, made Irene nervous. She felt sweat drip down between her breasts and legs. She tapped her high-heeled toe on the cement floor as she rebuttoned her blouse. "Come on, come on!" she murmured.

Once inside the prison proper, the guard on duty directed her to the visitation area. He looked at her chest as if he recognized her and almost said something, but then looked quizzically at her face and shook his head.

Georgie was waiting for her at a conference table.

She sat down and smiled at him. Her preference would have been to jump his bones, but in her role of Clare O'Toole, attorney-at-law, she had to rein in the sexual heat.

He smiled back at her. "Attorney O'Toole," Then in a much quieter voice, "You look fuckin' awesome, babe. I barely recognized you. The hair and all."

She reached into her "briefcase"—nothing more than a large pleather purse—and withdrew some papers. "I wanted to go over some of these notes with you before you sign." She watched the guard across the room avert his eyes from her body to something less interesting, like cleaning his nails. "Just read through this paragraph here," and she tapped the page with a high-gloss red talon. "If you have any questions, we can discuss things when you're done."

Georgie knew that the entire paragraph was in code.

He was prepared.

After reading the page he looked up at Irene. His smile told her all she needed to know.

He got the message.

He leaned back in his chair and spoke loud enough for the guard to hear. "I think it's all pretty clear, Attorney O'Toole." He winked. "I can sign now."

Fifteen minutes later Irene drove out of the parking lot and down the highway for ten miles. She pulled into a McDonald's; ordered a Big Mac, fries and a Diet Coke; then pulled her car into an empty space near the dumpsters.

While she ate, she withdrew the meaningless papers from her briefcase with Georgie's signature on the bottom and shredded them into small pieces. Then she stuffed them into the container for the Big Mac, shoved the uneaten portion of the sandwich on top of the shredded papers, added the uneaten fries, and crammed the whole wad into the dumpster when no one was looking.

She left the parking lot and headed to her dingy one-bedroom apartment in Miami, dreaming about her future.

Three months and Georgie would be a free man. She would no longer have to work at The Upside Diner as head waitress. And even though she had made many friends with her "regulars," she was ready to hand her crown to the next in line.

No, she was ready for the next chapter in her life.

The embedded code that Georgie had signed was simple: Pagoda Motel. Heatherton County, Florida. Under refrigerator. First cabin on right. About four feet under.

A cool three million.

Monday, September 19, 1980
The Pagoda Motel
Heatherton County, Florida

The beach weather for mid-September was glorious, with no clouds to obscure an azure blue sky. A light breeze blew in from the northwest, keeping the surf calm and peaceful. Lorna adjusted the towel on the back of her beach lounger. "This is just what the doctor ordered."

Doreen, a *Motorcycle Mechanics* magazine open in her lap, nodded. "Couldn't be better."

"So, tell me more about your brother, Georgie," Lorna said.

Doreen slid her sunglasses down from her head to her nose and closed the magazine. "Well, what do you wanna know?"

"You said he was named after your father's brother?"

"Yeah, well, see, my father had a younger brother named Georgie. He died of pneumonia when he was only, like, ten or something. Weak lungs from birth. My father never got over losing him, so after I came along, he wanted a boy. He got my mother pregnant right away. He had this harebrained idea that if he acted quickly, the next-born would be a boy."

"Hmph. Interesting concept, but I'm not sure it's accurate."

"Well, the fact was that she had a boy."

"Coincidence, I'm sure."

"So, anyhow, my brother Georgie." Doreen sighed and said nothing for a moment. "Let's just say that after dad died he just … turned."

"Turned?"

Doreen nodded. "Yeah. He was a sensitive kid. It was hard for him to make friends. He kept to himself a lot and appeared shy. He liked to draw. He used anything around him to make pictures. He colored the walls of the house with crayons and finger paints, and my mother would have a coronary. She managed to get him to draw in sketchbooks. That seemed to help the wall situations. My father called him a sissy. He wanted a son that would follow in his footsteps."

Lorna nodded. "Ah. A son to carry on his legacy."

"Yeah. So when Dad got gunned down, Georgie turned into a punk. But he wasn't street smart; he just wanted to look the part. To make a long story short, he started defacing public property with spray paint. I think he figured that for all the years my parents stopped him from painting on the walls of the house he could spread his talents on the sides of buildings. He used to go out in the middle of the night and not come back until mid-morning. My mother didn't know what to do with him, and after dad died and we moved down to Miami to live with Uncle Vinnie, he got worse. He got caught doing petty stuff, like stealing spray cans of paint, art supplies, that sort of thing. He didn't have the balls to do big thefts, only stuff he needed for his artwork."

"Why didn't your mother or Uncle Vinnie help him out by buying him supplies? It would have been a lot easier don't you think?"

"Because my mother was more concerned with finding a new man, and Uncle Vinnie and his sons wanted Georgie to learn the ropes of the business."

"Business? You mean—"

"Running the service stations Vinnie owned."

Lorna left it at that. She redirected. "Georgie has all this talent and nowhere to put it, so he steals his supplies and paints on the sides of buildings. I assume he got caught and that's why he's in prison?"

"Well, it's a minimum-security prison really. He's not a hardened criminal. Just a kid who grew up expressing himself ... with paints."

Lorna shook her head. "Sounds like he got a bum deal. Seems like a talented guy. Did he have a job, a way to pay for his supplies?"

"Never held anything down. Too unfocused. He's done

some small jobs, like in a restaurant kitchen, but never really showed any desire to learn a trade. He's a talented kid who got pretty screwed up along the way." Doreen sighed again and shook her head. "His graffiti stuff is amazing. I was, well, *am*, in awe of how he can see something small and make it big. I mean, do you know how hard it is to paint something on the side of a building and make it look real?"

Lorna thought of the beautiful mural on her kitchen wall painted by a mother who loved her family and expressed it with paints so long ago. "I guess it's all about perspective and space."

"Yeah, like ..." Doreen grabbed her book. "See this picture on the cover here?"

Lorna nodded.

"He could re-create this on the side of a building to scale, know what I mean?"

"I think so. It takes talent to do that. Sounds like true art."

"It *is* art. It's called tagging. But ... after the fourth time Georgie got caught the judge decided to rehabilitate him at Redhook."

"Redhook?"

"A min-sec prison just outside of Miami. They teach the guys how to make useful things for society. Like, y'know, license plates and stuff ..." she trailed off, seeming disgusted.

"So, how is that considered rehab? I mean, just because they take away his tools doesn't mean they take away his talent. What makes them think that when he gets out, he's going to revert to sketch pads? It seems that this ... tagging ... is his emotional balance. Why didn't your parents encourage him?"

Doreen sighed. "Lorna, boys in the family grew up to run the family businesses. Period. Not to explore talents such as art."

"What a complete waste."

"I know. The kid is talented and has no direction." She looked off toward the horizon, and her shoulders slumped. "And I was no help either. After watching Dad get gunned down, I just ran. I was lost, too. We had to go along with the family plans and move from New York to Florida. We had to leave our lives behind, and quick. And when I got to Florida, Vinnie tried teaching *me* the business—as per my father's wishes, mind you, because he knew Georgie couldn't handle it—but I wanted nothing to do with it. All I wanted to do was learn how to fix engines and build stuff. I hung out with my cousins at the shop after school and learned the trades. I had no social life. I just wanted out. So, when I was old enough to get my inheritance, I built my Harley to spec and took off. Georgie chose to stick around and run with some punks, but mostly he wanted to express himself, and the only way he could do that was to tag. No one understood him; no one wanted to deal with him."

Lorna had seen some impressive graffiti art in her time—and not just in the United States. When she traveled through Europe with her family, some of the world's oldest cities flowered with colorful designs on bridges, viaducts, and buildings. "Maybe he can have a future in some way ..."

"If my parents had accepted his talent instead of following the fucked-up family tradition of the business, he might not be locked up today for the stupid shit he chose to do instead," Doreen said.

Lorna added, "He doesn't sound like a criminal. His only crime was trying to pursue a desire."

"Yeah, he had to do it on the sly and steal to get what he needed to feel satisfied. Kind of like a drug addict without the drugs."

"I'd be thankful for that if I were a parent."

"Yeah. Well, when Dad died, he spiraled out of control and sealed up his heart. Locked it all up."

Lorna stroked Doreen's arm lightly. "Kind of like his big sister, right?"

"Maybe something like that." Doreen leaned over the arm of the chair and brought her lips toward Lorna's face, but instead looked over Lorna's head and murmured, "We got company."

Anya Catalvo, Lorna's Mexican live-in caretaker, strode up to them. Doreen cleared her throat and pulled back, bringing her reading material back up to her eyes again.

"Oh, hello, Misses."

Lorna shaded her eyes, "Hi! You going to join us for a little relaxation?"

"Oh, no, not today. I came to tell you there is someone in the lobby who is asking to see you. She did not, well, would not give me her name. She said she was an old, old friend of yours, had not seen you for many years, from up north and wanted to surprise you."

Lorna's hackles rose immediately. "Oh? What did she look like?"

Anya shrugged. "Like a woman, really."

"Okay. Well."

Doreen asked, "What's up, hon? Do you think you know who it is?"

Lorna felt her pulse quicken. It couldn't be. "What did you tell her, Anya?"

"I told her you were getting some relaxation with Miss Doreen. She asked me to tell her how to get to where the beach was, and I thought maybe I should tell you first. She is wearing, like, high heels and a skirt. So I told her to sit in the lobby, and I brought her some lemonade. Then I came down here to tell you of her arrival."

Doreen asked, "Do you think it's an old friend from college or something?"

"Yeah, from school."

Doreen cocked her head. She studied Lorna for a few moments and then seemed to catch on. "Ah, oh shit."

"Yeah, oh shit."

Anya said, "You want me to tell her you are busy just now and maybe to come back later?"

Lorna stared out into the vast Atlantic. Crystalline whitecaps flowed carelessly to the beach, the surf lapping quietly over the shells and debris. The sun warmed her shoulders. She was just starting to relax after the crazy week of renter calls.

She sighed. "No, I'll be right up."

She felt Doreen's hand on her arm. The warmth of it made her feel safe. She stood up, slipped on a tank top and beach wrap, then leaned over to kiss Doreen. She whispered, "I've got this."

As she and Anya took off on the path to the motel, she thought, *I hope.*

Lorna knew it was Jeanie, her first true love from high school seventeen years ago. Jeanie Doyle, the first and only person who had wakened Lorna's youthful heart with a seismic shift, filling it with magic and then taking it away in the blink of an eye.

In the years since Jeanie, Lorna's relationships had fallen flat because no one measured up. No one made her feel like she did when she fell in love with Jeanie. No one had the chance.

Lorna *felt* it in every bone of her body. Her heart skipped, and her head swam as she strode with Anya up to the main building.

Anya had to run to keep pace with her. "Slow down, Miss," she panted. "This is how we will get heart attacks! It's like you are on a commission or something."

Anya's misnomers never failed to make her smile.

Lorna stopped to look at her. "I've got it from here, Anya."

"All right, Miss. If you need me, I will be right around the corner."

Anya split off toward the cabin she shared with her husband, Milton—the other half of the caretaking team.

The front door loomed. Lorna hadn't had time to process this. With sweaty palms, she opened the door and entered the building.

And there she was. A beige suit jacket was laid neatly over the back of the couch where she was sitting. Lorna walked around to the front of her and stared. She whispered, "Jeanie?"

Jeanie nodded. "It's me. In the flesh!"

Lorna managed to shake her head slowly. "I ... don't even know what to say."

Jeanie snorted lightly, "Hello would be a good start."

Lorna responded immediately. "Hello."

Jeanie appraised her. "You look ... incredible, Lorna. Wow."

Lorna was still staring at Jeanie's face. God, how she loved that face. The long angular nose, the thin but shapely lips. So many hours spent so many years ago tracing her features with her fingertips, her lips. Now Jeanie looked thin, almost frail.

Lorna finally swallowed. "Thank you."

Jeanie patted the empty space on the couch next to her. "Come sit."

Lorna chose instead the chair opposite her. "How did you find me? I mean, what brought you down here?"

"I know you're shocked to see me after all these years."

"Yes I am."

"Lorna, I have so much to talk to you about, so much to say. I don't know where to begin. I wasn't sure how to contact you but, as fate would have it, I was having lunch with my daughter Lily, she's fifteen you see, about a week ago at our favorite offbeat restaurant—remember Tommy's?"

Lorna nodded.

"It was like *that* but in downtown Philly, where we live."

"I see."

Jeanie talked quickly and gesticulated with her hands. "Anyhow, I guess Lily inherited her bohemian edge from me. God knows she didn't get it from Kurt." She chuckled.

Lorna smiled, trying to keep up, but felt an internal heat rise from her belly into her chest and up through her shoulders.

"Well, Lily was reading *Lesbian Connection* when I arrived."

Lorna's eyebrows rose.

Jeanie saw Lorna's reaction and added quietly, "Lily thinks she might have lesbian tendencies. She's not sure how she feels about boys and all, but I ... um ... sorry. I'm getting sidetracked here. Anyhow she showed me your ad."

"Really." A statement more than a question.

Jeanie cleared her throat, her neck beet red. When Jeanie got uncomfortable with a conversation, her neck gave her away. She said, "I told her about us ... you and I ... a while ago when she confided to me that she had feelings for her best friend, Andrea. She took an interest in my ... our ... experience together in high school and asked me what your name was. She recognized the name in the *Connection* and asked me if you were the one and the same. I read the ad you placed, looked at your picture, and told her it was indeed you. She thinks you are very pretty."

"Well, that's nice. Thank you."

"But that isn't my agenda for coming to see you."

Lorna nodded without saying anything. Her intestines signaled a possible run to the bathroom. She tried to calm herself down.

Jeanie looked Lorna square in the eye. "I'm just ... of course now that I'm here, right in front of you, my strength seems to be petering out." After a few beats she asked, "Are you still angry with me?" Her voice was quiet, timid.

"I was."

Jeanie leaned in and blurted, "It's wasn't very easy for me either, you know."

Lorna studied her. "Why now?"

Jeanie looked directly into Lorna's eyes—an action that had typically disarmed Lorna in the past, but this time Lorna waited for an explanation without getting lost in Jeanie's pale blue eyes.

"Because for seventeen years I've done battle with my emotions. After I got back from the coast, from school, I met Kurt. We got married six months later because I was pregnant with Lily." Jeanie sighed deeply, looking away from Lorna. She fidgeted with the hem of her skirt, then said, "Maybe this was a mistake, coming here."

"What were you hoping for?"

"Resolution?"

"Absolution?" Lorna quickly countered.

"Probably both. I don't want you to hate me for the rest of our lives."

"I don't hate you, Jeanie." Lorna looked down at her bare tanned feet, hoping the answer would be there, somewhere in-between her red painted toes. It wasn't. But the pause gave her a chance to put the next few sentences together.

She looked up. "I was terribly hurt. After I found out about you and Aaron—from your mother no less—and that the two of you …" She swallowed hard. "God, you took all the beauty we created out of my heart without so much as a warning. You drained the colors and senses right out of my soul. I gave everything to you. You had it all." Lorna's eyes misted. She turned her head away from Jeanie and tried to stare at something else in the room. She would not give Jeanie the benefit of her tears.

Jeanie cleared her throat, trying to maintain a sense of calm. She also fought down the emotional wedge that simmered and threatened to erupt in her throat. She promised herself she would not cry or buckle. During the drive to Heatherton County that morning, she had played through several scenarios of how this visit might turn out. But it wasn't going according to plan. She'd hoped Lorna might be more receptive.

"Okay."

Lorna continued. "Why did you leave me? Us? Why didn't you talk about it with me when it happened? You just …" She caught a sob in her throat and reached for the Kleenex on one of the end tables. "… hung me out to dry. Most times I couldn't even breathe, and I had to fake it at home. I had to live my life as if nothing had happened." She blew her nose and tried to keep the years of pent-up emotion in check. She struggled.

Jeanie swallowed and reached for a tissue herself. "I know. I'm sorry. It was hard on me, too. I was scared. Scared of the lesbian lifestyle. And the labels. The looks. The scorn from everyone at school. Aaron provided a safety net for me."

Lorna said, "So you took what was so sacred between us and labeled it? We were *in love* with each other, and nothing else mattered!"

Jeanie sat up a little straighter now, her voice carrying more conviction. "Oh, come *on*, Lorna. What in the hell did we know back then? Hmm? Life mattered! I mean, look how hard it was for us to integrate the *us* into our lives? We…we had to be sly and secretive with our family. Our friends understood the free love thing only so far. My parents were cool but to a point. I think they saw this young love as a phase. And I was going to go to school in California, and you were heading to Case."

Lorna said, "I compared everyone to you afterward. No one had a chance."

Jeanie sighed, resigned.

They sat in uncomfortable silence looking at one another.

Lorna realized something quite clearly, and it made her sad. The spark was gone. All that was left was rawness. Lorna did not know if she was glad Jeanie had come to her or not. She always dreamed of running into her somewhere on the street or in a restaurant or... She never even knew Jeanie had moved away from Cleveland. She'd had her shields in place. But now the years had clearly defined them apart.

Jeanie said, "I will always love you, Lorna. You were my first, and there is nothing that compares with that."

Lorna nodded. Her heart now was surprisingly calm. A little heavy but calm. "I will always love you as well," she said quietly.

After another long moment of silence, Jeanie tried to be upbeat. "So, what brought you to Florida and this?" She looked around the lobby. "Last I heard, from the high school alumni newsletter that is, you were lawyering in Cleveland."

"It's a long story."

"So, give me the short version?"

What Lorna wanted to do was to tell Jeanie to hit the road. But she tried to keep it conversational. "Well, after Dad died late last year—"

Jeanie sat up. "Your father died? My God, Lorna, what? How?"

"Right in the middle of a board meeting. Heart attack. He went quickly."

Jeanie's eyes softened, "Oh honey, I am so sorry. He seemed like such a healthy man."

Lorna wanted to get back on track. "After he died, I felt like I needed a change in my life. I was bored and fed up with work, my love life was going nowhere, and the winters in

Cleveland were killing me."

What Lorna did not expound upon was the bittersweet relief she felt when her father died. It released her from a life of rote expectations from a man who did not accept failure of any kind. It gave her the "out" she had dreamt about since becoming junior partner at the same law firm her father used.

Lorna explained, "I was on the Board for The Arts Council of Greater Cleveland, and after hearing story after story about how these very talented people couldn't get ahead because of monetary setbacks, I decided to take matters into my own hands. I hired a real estate broker who found me this property, and I decided to start the collective—the one you read about in the paper—here at the motel."

Jeanie shook her head slowly. "Wow. You never cease to amaze me. You just reinvented yourself like ..." She snapped her fingers. "... like that?"

"It was time. I wasn't getting any younger."

"Thirty-five is hardly over the hill, Lorn."

Lorna shrugged. "Well, it was time."

Jeanie asked, "Did you ever think you'd be doing this?"

Lorna chuckled, "You sound like my best friend, Avril. She thought I was nuts for wanting to do this. Thought I was having a midlife crisis. The opportunity presented itself, and I grabbed it. The cost of the property was dirt cheap. The time was right."

Jeanie remarked, "And that garden out there, the one from the picture in the paper. Just gorgeous! Was it here when you bought the place?"

"Ah, no. It was an old tennis court, not very appealing to the eye. We decided to dig it up and turn it into the garden you see now."

The front door opened, and Doreen stuck her head in. "Hi there."

Saved by the gorgeous brunette. "Come on in, babe."

Doreen entered a bit gingerly. "Well, I don't want to interrupt anything here."

Jeanie turned to look at her, then at Lorna.

Doreen approached Lorna and put her hand on her shoulder. The connection was immediate, and the gesture grounded Lorna. "Jeanie, this is Doreen. Doreen, Jeanie."

Doreen reached across the table for Jeanie's hand. "Nice to meet ya. I've, ah, heard a lot about you."

Jeanie nodded. "Same here. Well, not that I've heard a lot about you, but nice to meet you."

Well, there they were.

Now what? thought Lorna. She stood up.

Jeanie picked up on the signal and stood up too. She gathered her suit jacket and purse and said, "Well, I think I'm going to check out the town of St. Augustine. I've heard it's a quaint lovely place. Maybe get a bite to eat."

Lorna said, "It is. Just head out over the bridge and take a right onto the main road. You'll see signs."

Doreen and Lorna walked Jeanie outside and to the door of her rental car.

Jeanie stopped before opening the door to the car. She said, "The garden is more exquisite in person, Lorna. It's truly peaceful and inviting." She looked around and sighed. "It's pretty heavenly here. So rustic. Homey. Congratulations on your endeavor. I can't help but feel a bit jealous of your surroundings." She opened the door to her car and deposited her suit jacket and purse on the passenger side seat. As she got into the car, she said, "Thank you for seeing me."

They watched her drive out of the turnaround and take a right onto Bridge Street.

Doreen asked, "You okay, honey?"

Lorna took in a deep breath and felt her eyes well up. She could barely talk. "Hollow. I feel hollow right now. Maybe seeing her was supposed to put closure on the whole thing. Maybe it's more about *that* than anything else."

Lorna burrowed her face into Doreen's shoulder. The tears ran freely. It felt good to release the darkness. "It's right here, right now, that I feel the safest."

Doreen held her quietly.

Monday, September 19, 1980
Red Hook Minimum Security Prison
Red Hook County
Miami

Georgie went back to his cell and pulled one of his sketchbooks from a small shelf, opening it to a blank page.

He picked up a charcoal pencil from the metal desk and drew some lines on the scratchy white paper. He looked up through his window and sighed. Some of the guys were playing basketball in the yard. Others were sitting reading, staring out into nowhere or chatting with one another. It all looked so normal, almost like a college campus, except for the guards standing at every entrance/exit to the building, and the bars on the windows.

Georgie was a good inmate. He did what he was told, worked hard in the kitchen, and kept to himself.

He filled almost thirty sketchbooks during his incarceration. He fought the impulse to use his charcoal and watercolor chalks on the walls because he knew the penalty would be scrubbing every visible surface in the joint twice over or, worse, they would take his supplies away.

His sketchbooks were his sanity. The prison screws were lenient, and a few of them even took interest in his work. But for the most part he kept to himself and lived within the confines of his real and art-inspired world.

Three more months and the world would be his once again.

He pictured the cabin at the Pagoda Motel. The very place where his grandfather, Gino DiLarusso, had governed and made big decisions about "the family." Where he had supposedly hid three million dollars in cash. Which supposedly no one had retrieved, according to his uncle, who knew quite a bit about the family history.

It was during a visit from Irene that Georgie had hatched the plan. It was a Saturday afternoon in late July. Irene had shared a conversation she'd had with one of her regulars at The Upside Diner. His name was Vinnie Regazzini.

"That's my fuckin' uncle," Georgie informed her.

Her eyes lit up. "Your fuckin' uncle?"

"Yeah! Gino DiLarusso was my grandfather."

"Holy shit. Do you know about the money buried at some motel up north?"

"What motel? What money?"

"Vinnie tells me stuff all the time. Big stories—I don't know if they're true or not. But seems like there were some big shots in your family, Georgie."

"There were. My father got shot after someone poisoned Gino because he hit a bunch of guys on our side of the family 'cause they were skimmin' off the top. I guess the story goes that the son gets hit too. So my dad got it one night while we were having pizza. My sister watched it too. It was pretty bad."

"Aw, honey."

"Anyhow, tell me more about what he said. About the money and being buried somewhere?"

"It's probably nothing big. He said that Gino used a safe house up near St. Augustine. Some motel with some cabins, off the beaten path. Seems as though he had lots of meetings there, made lots of plans."

Georgie urged her on, "Yeah, well, what about the money?"

"Vinnie said that he was pretty sure Gino buried a lot of cash, but after he died the guys had to find a new location for their operations, so I guess they all split."

"But if there's all that money there, why hasn't someone gone and gotten it yet?" He tried to think back to when he lived with Vinnie, whether Vinnie had ever mentioned this story to him. He couldn't remember specifics, wasn't really interested in the mob stuff.

Irene had shrugged. "Like I said, Vinnie's probably tellin' a tall tale. He likes to brag to me. I think he likes my boobs."

"He'd better keep his dirty old man hands off your boobs. Those are mine."

Irene had smirked. "Last I knew they were mine, but you can check them out of the library every once in a while."

Georgie said, "I think you need to get more information from Vinnie about this money. If it's *really* true and no one's taken it, then, what's to say we can't?"

Irene smiled, "You might be on to somethin'. I'll pump him for more info."

A few weeks later, Irene had shared more intel with Georgie, and they'd hatched a plan.

Irene was to gather the exact location of the motel and where Vinnie thought the money might be buried. If she had to use her boobs to get more intel out of Vinnie, then she would. Then she would get the info to Georgie via a coded message.

Which they did this morning.

The plan was to hit the motel cabin late in January. Irene would first drive up there and pretend to be interested in renting one of the cabins.

Irene was also in charge of gathering all the tools they would need to get in and out of the cabin pronto. She bought the shovels—two small spades with collapsible handles—a pry-bar, two small flashlights, and dark clothing.

Georgie sketched the cabin as he thought it might look. He reached for a red marker and wrote on the side of the cabin *Georgie and Irene were here*. Then, in smaller letters, *and now we're gone!*

Ellen Bennett

The Ladies of Pagodaville

The Ladies of Pagodaville

ONE
SoHo, New York City
September 26, 1980

PARIS KATHERINE (PK) TODD

PK, barely awake after a late-night gig in the Village, stumbled from her bed to the door. "Jeez! Who is it?"

"It's me, open the damn door!" It was Melanie, the bass player for PK's band, The Sweet, and she did not sound happy.

PK's head ached and her stomach roiled as she unlocked several latches. Too much crappy beer from the crappy bar at the crappy venue.

Melanie strode in and tossed her jacket haphazardly on an amplifier.

PK attempted to run her fingers through a tangle of shoulder-length brown/blond hair without success. She rubbed her deep-set brown eyes with the heels of her hands, sighing while she felt, more than watched, Melanie pace.

"What, Mel?" she managed to say.

"Are you really going to do it? Leave the band? Go to effin' Florida? Have you discussed this with Jon? And why did I have to find out about it from Cass?"

"Yeah, I have," PK answered her. "I've discussed this with Jon. It's *my* life, Mel. I need a change of surroundings."

PK shuffled into her dingy galley kitchen in her overpriced under-cared-for fifth-story walk-up in SoHo. She needed coffee. Bad.

When she had moved into the apartment eight years prior, she was glad to be out of her parents' home in Westchester. Glad to finally have a space of her own despite her mother's guttural comments about it being the hovel of the century.

She used the space by filling it not with furniture, but with musical equipment. Her sparse living fundamentals suited her just fine. It was all about the music. She had goals. And what other friends considered necessities were merely wasted dollars in PK's eyes. She had had enough overabundance growing up.

The money she made from gigs and her full-time job at Jimmy's Harborside as a line cook did not support the better things in life. But she had acquired two beautiful guitars, one acoustic and one electric, which she used at all the gigs. Her guitars were extensions of her hands, and her voice carried her soul flawlessly to whoever listened.

Melanie stopped pacing long enough to ask, "Why do you have to move all the way down to Florida? I mean, what gives, Paris?" She stomped her way from the tiny kitchen to the tiny living room and back again, arms crossed tightly in front of her.

The last thing PK wanted to do was to justify her feelings to Melanie, or anyone for that matter, about leaving New York City. But she needed to say something, anything to get Mel to stop her incessant pacing.

She reached for a mug from the rusted dish drainer. "It won't be forever. I need some time to work on new material. I can't do it here. I need a change of scenery, Mel."

"But don't you know we are replaceable? Jon can find another band in five minutes. We haven't exactly hit the big time yet."

What PK did not share with Mel was that she and Jon had worked out a solo contract.

Jon understood her. He had been following her career from the moment he'd heard her at a venue in upstate New York. His job was to scout new talent for Sable Records, one of the leading rock-and-roll labels in the country, and when he heard PK's throaty, edgy yet discernible, voice laced with heartfelt lyrics, he knew she was going to be someone for him to develop.

Jon understood that she needed time to re-create herself. They had talked long and hard about what the future might hold and decided that taking time would be in both their best interests. He wanted good material from her, no matter how long it took.

"Look, Mel, I'm going to make this move. I need to get out of the city.

Melanie finally stopped pacing. "And what about us?"

PK sighed. "I know. We have to talk."

"You're fucking me over, aren't you?"

PK tried to defend herself, but it came out more as a shrug. The truth was that PK was ready to move on.

"Don't fucking shrug your shoulders at me! *Say something!*"

"Mel, really. Keep your voice down."

Melanie shook her head. "You know, for all your bravado on stage, for all your kick-ass guitar licks and hair swinging and lyrics of steel, you're a real pussy."

"Enough, Mel. Lighten up."

"Lighten up?" Mel moved up close to PK. "Maybe you should face the truth, Paris."

"What are you talking about?"

She moved closer. "Three months ago, you and I were tight, we were friends, and we were writing killer songs. We had a real connection on stage. And then I made the mistake of letting your charm and passion take over my heart. Three months, Paris. We moved like one on stage. And off? The sex was amazing, your passion was crazy deep. But then, you just detached ... with napalm."

"Mel, come on. I'm not—"

"Whatever you're going to say, zip it. You're twenty-six, but you have the emotional attention span of a seventeen-year-old boy."

PK crossed her arms in front of her chest. "And you? You're so evolved at thirty?"

"I've played my love life in real time. You don't. Here's what you do. You find someone new, a pretty thing. But she can dance and sucks up to you. She's enamored and full of inspiration. And when your creative inspiration peters out, she's history."

"Wait a minute—"

"No, your time is up, Paris. You and I *had* a true connection. I wasn't just some perky fan thinking you were the next best thing to her vibrator."

PK walked away from her. "See? You and I should've just remained friends. I don't need this shit."

Melanie sighed and dropped her shoulders. "Yeah. You're just not going to get this, Paris."

"Get what, Mel?"

Melanie regarded her. "Maybe one day you'll wonder why your life is missing something. You got your music and your future, but …"

Melanie reached for her beat-up leather band jacket and shrugged it on. She said resignedly, "Well, good luck with the move, Paris. Maybe you'll meet someone down in Florida who can give you a run for your money and toss you aside when the passion fizzles out." She took a deep breath and added, "I assume you'll grace us with your presence at the gig tonight?"

"Of course, I'll be there."

PK was the front woman of her own band.

She could do it without them.

Melanie muttered, "I just hope you can keep a clear conscience about what you're doing to us as a band."

Melanie looked at PK, waiting for something. A nod, a hug, an acknowledgment, something.

PK had nothing for her.

TWO
Santa Fe, New Mexico
September 27, 1980

MARIELLA 'MARI' VASQUEZ

After she closed the side doors of her VW van, Mari took one more look around the lovely garden and patio of what had been her home for the last six years. She would miss the brilliant colors against the southwest skies, the heady aromas of cactus flowers, and the vast expanse of desert, framed by the Sandia Mountains in the distance. She would miss the clean air that was New Mexico.

She'd stowed some food in a cooler on the front seat of the van and had checked the tires one more time. She had rearranged the back of the vehicle to accommodate a makeshift bed for her travels, with her earthly belongings off to one side. All she really needed was her electric typewriter, plenty of paper, her journals, and her clothes. Other than that, she left the furniture, kitchen appliances, and major artwork for Lonnie to deal with.

She wanted very little of their life together in the way of material goods. There were plenty of shards left over from Lonnie's infidelity without the clutter of what once was.

In her jeans pocket was the soft, worn drawstring sack containing two glass angels given to her by her Nani, to keep her safe in her life. Mari cherished them even if their powers seemed to have waned over the years.

It was time to go.

Forty-year-old Mariella Vasquez was quiet and unassuming. She was small in stature and nondescript in physical beauty but had deep brown eyes that were at times soft and gentle, and at other times full of fire.

Her smile, however, was her draw. White and wide, surrounded by thick dark red lips. People fell into her smile.

She wore her long, thick dark hair in a braid to keep it out of her eyes and off her face. When she worked at her typewriter, she could have no distractions.

When Mari had read the ad in the *Lesbian Connection*, advertising for artists, musicians, and writers at The Pagoda Motel in Heatherton County, Florida, she'd called the proprietor immediately.

She had introduced herself as a published writer.

The proprietor, Lorna Hughes, seemed very interested.

Half an hour later, and after Lorna had explained the concept of the motel, the logistics and rent, Mari knew she would go.

On her way out of town, Mari stopped at the post office to send the check for the first month's rent, and a copy of her novel, *A Woman from Brazil,* to Lorna Hughes.

Lorna expected the check, not the book.

Mari thought that would be a good way to introduce herself.

She then left town and entered the highway to head south.

Then east for 1,600 miles.

She did not look back.

THREE
Gloucester, Massachusetts
September 28, 1980

ALICE 'LUCKY' PUNSTON

Alice took her tabletop easel, collapsible chair, two five-by-seven watercolor paper cards, a jug of water, some small rags, and a few paints out to the pier.

The sky held no contrast—just a milky white backdrop and a few scattered boats floating listlessly on the murky bay water. She set her gear up on a small wooden barrel that served as her workspace.

Alice had been working on a set of greeting cards for a small outfit in Boston and needed a few more watercolors to finish the pack. Commercial work like this wasn't her gig, but she needed the money.

She painted in robot mode, her mind on the recent phone call she'd had with a woman in Florida named Lorna Hughes, who was looking for renters at her motel.

When Alice had seen the ad in the *Lesbian Connection*, she jumped. It seemed too good to be true. A haven for artists and the like. Individual cabins, cheap rent, fully furnished. What could go wrong?

She could pack her earthly belongings in her station wagon.

It was just the kick she needed to get out of the bitter cold and depressing winters of New England, out from under the collapsed bridge of her recent life.

And with her creativity at a standstill, a change of scenery was the next logical choice.

Alice Punston had been an artist from childhood. Her mother, Louise, used to tease her. "Whenever you had something in your hand that could be used on the walls of this house, there was no stoppin' you!" And the media ranged from chalk to spaghetti sauce, pencils and peanut butter, finger paints, magic markers, and cake frosting, to name a few.

Her parents realized that the best way to detour frequent interior renovations was to equip their daughter with washable paints, crayons and *lots* of sketch pads. Her father, a print specialist at *The Boston Globe*, brought home blank newsprint papers much to the glee of his young artist in residence.

Alice did not have many friends growing up. She was teased because she was taller than children in her age group. She was thin, birdlike, pale. They called her an ostrich, a giraffe or, worse, a ghost.

She kept to herself knowing that no one understood her except for her parents. And when her younger sister, Cora came along, her parents transferred their attentions to the baby, who was born with cognitive and developmental issues.

Alice had become a latchkey kid by the time she was twelve, fending for herself the best way she could.

In high school, she did her best to keep her grades up, but it was at the art studio at Gloucester Island High School where she excelled, came alive.

Her style was not like anything the teachers had seen before. There was a bold yet gentle flow of lines and color to her painting. If the class was working on a still life, Alice painted the lesson as required. But instead of the given backdrop, she might insert a gritty downtown building, or a pier, or a fishing boat. Something to unbalance the subject and cause the eye to see the subject as the backdrop and the backdrop as the focal point.

Claire Estherhaus, an art teacher at the high school, watched Alice closely. She saw something very different and special in Alice's expression. While her other students did the work as was instructed, Alice usually took each assignment to higher levels—far beyond the comprehension of her classmates.

Claire inquired, "Where does your eye go after looking at the subject? How does the backdrop relate?"

Alice answered, "It's a story, really. It's not just a vase full of flowers. It's the story behind it."

Claire regarded the assignment Alice had finished. "So, when you see something, it's not really just the subject?"

"No, never."

"Do you write stories, too?"

"No, I get too frustrated with words."

Claire was instrumental in propelling Alice to apply to Williams College in Williamstown, Massachusetts, where the art program was one of the top five in the nation. The entrance competition was fierce but while Claire watched and challenged Alice to keep learning her craft, she felt that Alice had a good shot at getting in.

She was accepted into the program.

Alice left home after graduating from high school, ready to dive headfirst into her studies.

Until many years later, an unfortunate situation occurred, bringing her back to her parents' home.

A voice from behind her startled her out of her thoughts. "Hey, girl."

Barb Hastings, a recent ex-lover of Alice's—one of the few who managed to maintain a friendship with her—put a hand upon Alice's shoulder and jiggled a bag.

When Alice smelled the contents, she cooed, "You brought me coffee! How did you know?"

"Silly question." Barb kissed the top of Alice's head, then set the bag next to Alice's little stool.

"Are you still goin' into Boston today?"

"Yeah, gotta finish this last one, and then I'll take off."

Alice reached into the bag, feeling the familiar warmth of the lidded cardboard cup and the small lump next to it, which she knew to be a blueberry muffin.

Barb looked at what Alice was working on. "I like this, but I don't see a bicycle on the pier."

"That's because I needed something to offset this colorless sky. You like the two-tone?"

"Love it." Then Barb added, "I'm surprised you didn't throw a dead body crashing up against the pier for added excitement."

"I would have, but gotta keep it sane for the commercial machine, know what I mean?"

"Jellybean. Yeah, I know what you mean."

Barb loved Alice's work. It could be macabre and sensuous at the same time. Or it could be kind of out there and seemingly pointless. But it always had a central theme. Even though sometimes it was a little more challenging to find that theme.

Their short-lived love relationship had morphed into a friendship when Alice admitted to Barb that she was closed off emotionally, that she had nothing to give. And Barb could not compete with the constant freight trains going through Alice's head.

Alice offered sincere friendship to Barb, who accepted that willingly. She loved Alice and saw her for the artist she was and might become.

Barb was also Alice's only friend in Gloucester.

Alice continued painting with one hand while blowing on her hot coffee with the other. Barb sat down on the uneven boards of the pier and crossed her legs, sipping her own beverage while looking out over the still waters of the bay. She inquired, "So, do you have any further thoughts about the Florida thing?"

Alice nodded. "I'm going to go."

Barb sighed. "Crap. That's what I thought you'd say."

Alice sipped her coffee. "I have to get out of here, Barb."

Barb put her hand on Alice's leg and squeezed, knowing full well why Alice had to leave Gloucester.

Barb's voice was quiet. "I know."

FOUR
September 28, 1980
Chicago, Illinois

LINDY SUTTON

David Stone faced Lindy from across the small cafe table, his eyes all squinty-like. "You're *really* going to go through with this, Lindy?"

She sipped her tea. Emphatically, in her best Southern drawl, she answered, "Why, yes. Yes, I am."

"You've got deadlines. How is that going to work with your deadlines?"

She regarded David, rolling her eyes. Sometimes he could be so annoying. "There is this new thing called the mail. What's got you so uptight? It's not like I'm moving to the moon, for Christ's sake."

He shifted in his chair. "I know, but what's going to inspire you in northern Florida? Heat? Humidity? Gulls?"

She pursed her lips. "I get my inspiration from interacting with people. This place in Florida, this motel with the cabins, is probably teeming with activity."

David sighed. "I know you'll meet your deadlines. You always do. But ..."

"I think my creativity will blossom there." She added, "And I'm quite used to the heat and humidity. Don't forget I was born and raised in Atlanta."

David scowled.

In an even deeper southern drawl, she daintily said, "Now, David, if you want to drop me as a client I would *showly* understand."

He sat up straighter in his chair, "Oh Christ, Lindy. Your

material is hot right now, and we can't afford to lose that momentum."

"What makes you think I'm going to stop? A change of scenery and pace will only make things more interesting don't you think?"

David tapped his fingertips on the tabletop. "Okay. So, how will you support yourself? Will you have to put your work aside to make ends meet? How will you get down there, and how will you get around?"

She frowned, then answered him. "What's with the third degree?"

David did not answer her. His nostrils flared.

She sighed. "I'm going to fly down to Atlanta, spend some time with my dad. He pulled my mom's Mustang out of storage and is getting it ready for the drive down to Florida. I have money in savings. The rent is dirt cheap and the cabin is furnished with the basics. So ... oh, and let's not forget those *hefty* royalty checks from you guys." This said with raised eyebrows.

David raised his hand, palm toward her. "I know ... I'm working on that."

Lindy muttered, "Uh huh." She took a bite of her scone.

She was *so* ready for this move down to Florida. Her creative fuel was starting to dip below the halfway mark. She prayed that the move to Florida would replenish the coffers.

Born into one of the wealthier families of the Deep South, Lindy was the eldest of three children to Horace and Vera Sutton.

Lindy had a zest for life. She embraced it with the innocence of a youngster. But because of her size—tall like her father and zaftig like her mother—growing up was a challenge among the slender, very lady-like southern belles.

Lindy had her mother's fair skin, almond-shaped hazel eyes, red hair, and broad encompassing smile. Her features were well placed. Her mother told her she was beautiful. Her father called her his princess.

But she was often ridiculed.

The girls might say, "Oh, she *has* to be funny to cover up for all that *fat*."

"That *hair*! Like a fire-breathing dragon!"

Or, in quieter tones, "She'll *never* snag a boy, she's too bossy and big."

For Lindy, snagging a boy was never going to be an issue because from a young age Lindy knew she liked girls better than boys. It wasn't a big epiphany, just something she felt in her heart.

When Lindy had finally admitted her proclivity to her parents during her senior year in high school, they were not surprised. They embraced her for being honest and forthright, but warned her that the world was not as loving and kind as they were, that she would have to stand tall and stick to her convictions.

During the summer between her junior and senior year at The Chicago School of Design, Lindy was blindsided with devastating news.

Vera had been diagnosed with Stage Four ovarian cancer.

No one caught it in time.

Lindy was adrift, the light drained from her soul.

She adored her mother. They were the best of friends.

The family and nurses rallied around Vera twenty-four-seven for five weeks until her death at home in August 1976.

Lindy put off going back to school until her father threw down the gauntlet and made her return for the winter session.

He'd said, "Your mother made me promise that you kids would continue your education and keep going from there."

Lindy had had no choice. She wanted to please her father and keep the request of her mother sacred, but she had no steam.

The breath went out of her. She missed her mother so much that she lost count of the days when she did not get out of bed, shower, change her clothes, or talk to anyone but her family.

She lost almost fifty pounds. Didn't care what she looked like. She saw her mother around every corner of the house, smelled her perfume, heard her dulcet tones in every room, and couldn't *look* at Vera's pride and joy, a midnight blue convertible Mustang named Midnight.

She had gone back to school reluctantly and had tried to get through her studies, tried to concentrate.

Her journaling reached new levels. She had one for depression, one for anger, one for when she smoked dope, one for when she had no one else to talk to.

She had gone to a therapist for a while, but even that proved directionless.

She knew she had to get through the pain on her own. She knew Vera would want her to live life to the fullest. So she had buckled down during her senior year and focused on her studies.

By the time she graduated from college, she decided to shop her graphic novel *More Than Just Clothes in THIS Closet* to several agents in town. Most of them turned her down because they weren't interested in shopping a comic book to publishers, but one agent, David Stone, found her work intriguing. He said it was fresh, funny, and encompassed all walks of life.

He and Lindy had met several times, and after three months McGill Publishing House signed her on.

Lindy remained in Chicago instead of going back Atlanta.

She found an apartment north of the city in the gay-friendly neighborhood of Halsted where she could supplement her monthly stipends from her father with her royalty checks from McGill.

But the city, her small circle of friends, the culture, it was getting old.

And, she was unequivocally and painfully single.

And still unequivocally and painfully angry at God for taking the one woman who had loved her unconditionally and who had left a Vera-sized hole in her heart.

David pushed his chair back, stood his six-foot frame up, and leaned on the back of his chair, facing her. He started to say something, then closed his mouth, sighing instead.

He turned on his heel and strode out of the coffeehouse.

Lindy had to smile. A gentle calm unfurled over her head like a soft blanket landing in slow motion.

She was okay with leaving the city.

She was okay with trying something new, something completely out of the norm. She was more than okay with gathering new fodder. It was time.

When she had talked with Lorna Hughes at The Pagoda Motel, she was certain the move was meant to be.

It would be good to get down south again. She missed her dad. And she'd be only one state away from him, not several.

And who knows what might transpire at this motel thing?

All she knew was that *nothing* was guaranteed in life.

Nothing.

FIVE
October 6, 1980
The Pagoda Motel

While Lorna and Doreen were getting ready for bed, Doreen asked Lorna, "So, are you all set for the ladies to arrive?"

Lorna set the book that had arrived earlier that day, on the bedside table.

Doreen asked, "What's that?"

Lorna handed it to her. "This is the book I was telling you about by one of the new tenants."

"Hm. *A Woman from Brazil* by Mariella Vasquez." Doreen turned it over to look at the picture of the author. "Spanish, huh?"

"American-born Latina. From New Mexico."

"Do you know what it's about?"

"No, not really."

"Well, that's pretty cool, having a published writer on board."

"It is. I can't wait to read it and meet her."

Doreen set the book back on the table. "Come here, babe. I want to talk to you about something."

Lorna scooted up close to her. "Ooh, sounds serious!"

"I talked to Vinnie earlier today. I think I should go down to Miami and pick up my gear, mostly tools and more clothes, and maybe a little bit of furniture. But what I was thinkin' was this. How about we—Milton and me that is—build a little garage for me to work in."

Lorna raised her eyebrows. "Um, sure. Where were you thinking of putting this garage?"

"Well, actually, the empty lot next to the motel. I checked on it earlier this week. It's a quarter acre. The city of

Heatherton owns it. They'd let it go for about five hundred."

Lorna had no idea Doreen was even thinking about this. "You surprise me at every corner."

Doreen sat up, excited. "It wouldn't be a big place, y' see. Just enough room to set up tools and a bay. I could work on everyone's car, or what have you."

"Are you going to buy the land?"

Doreen nodded her head. "I put some money down on it, but I wanted to talk to you first."

Lorna knew Doreen had a decent stash of money from her inheritance. Where she kept it and how she handled it wasn't something she readily disclosed. One side of Lorna did battle with how Doreen came about her money, and the other side reasoned no questions asked.

Lorna knew Doreen could read cars and engines with her eyes closed. It was uncanny how she could hear the slightest nuance of something amiss under the hood of a vehicle.

Lorna finally said, "I think it's a brilliant idea."

"You want to come down to Miami and meet Vinnie and the boys?"

"I have to be here. The ladies will be arriving over the next few days. When were you thinking of going?"

"Well, I was going to rent a van and drive it down. The sooner the better. Maybe Milton would like to go with me?"

"Ask him. The two of you are thick as thieves anyhow. He'd probably love the break."

"Can you spare him for a few days, a week maybe?"

"Of course. Anya and I have this."

"Well, I'm excited. How about you? You think this a good move?"

Lorna nodded. "Well, as Anya would say ..."—she gave it her best accent—"... yes, Miss, I think you are making a good movement."

Doreen chuckled, "Good impersonation. So I'll rent the truck and we'll leave in a few days. That sound okay?"

"Perfect."

They chatted for a little while longer before Doreen yawned and sprawled out under the sheets. "Goodnight, babe."

Lorna kissed Doreen lightly on the mouth, "Do you mind if I read for a while?"

Doreen rolled over. "Just come spoon when you're ready to fall asleep."

Lorna puffed and propped her pillows, then reached for the book from the nightstand.

She studied the front and back covers. She liked the front art. It resembled a block-like Picasso rendition of a woman leaning into and plucking guitar strings. The colors were browns and tans against an ecru background. The letter font in the title, like the artwork, was block-like, with the title of the book in a cascade down through the blocks. The author name on the very bottom in one line was bold, but smaller in point size.

Lorna was impressed.

She ran her fingers over the soft, slightly thick, cover paper and turned the book over. The head shot of Mariella Vasquez made her look kind, with her dark eyes and an engaging smile. Her hair was tied back, and she wore no makeup.

Lorna liked her immediately. She *looked* like a writer—plain yet intelligent. Straight on, no asides.

After reading the synopsis on the back cover, she knew she was going to be up late reading, if not all night. She was immediately drawn in from the description of the woman in the early 1930s who wanted to play flamenco guitar in a society where women did not do such things. Where women were married off to men before they were twenty, where women did not take women lovers.

The protagonist, Juliana Benedita, born to a father of business notoriety and a "society" mother, was an enigma to her parents from a young age …

When Lorna closed the book and laid it gently on her lap, it was almost seven o'clock in the morning.

With the story still so fresh in her mind, Lorna slipped out of bed and went downstairs. She made the coffee, waited until she could fill her mug, then quietly stepped out the back door and walked down to the beach, book in hand like a talisman.

A slim mist surrounded her as the sun peeked out over the ocean, the water calm, tide out. She loved this time of the day, as if no one else existed. She felt the immediate chill of the water on her insteps as she walked, and purposefully squeezed the cool sand between her toes.

She was lost in the world Vasquez created, lost in the character who struggled with having to live two lives.

In the aftermath of reading, Lorna found herself immersed in the descriptive imagery, in the flow of the words and action. She enjoyed how the information regarding flamenco guitar was woven into the narrative. She never knew how complex the art of playing the guitar was.

But more than anything, Lorna related to the protagonist with clarity. Even though the story evolved from the '30s to the '60s, the pathos was written in such a way as to progress effortlessly through the years.

When Lorna returned to the motel, Doreen was up and getting her coffee together.

"Hi, honey, nice walk? Did you sleep good?"

Lorna answered, showing Doreen the book. "I read this in one sitting."

"You were up all night?"

"All night."

Doreen went to hug Lorna. "You must be exhausted!"

"Not at all. If anything, I'm energized in a quiet kind of way. I don't think I've been so moved by a story."

"Wow. Maybe you can tell me about it. I'm not much of a reader."

A voice called out from the lobby, "Hola?"

Lorna returned the greeting, "Hey! We're in the kitchen."

Cheenah hugged Lorna and Doreen briefly. "Good morning. I was just going to go to the Farmers Market. Do you want anything?"

"Ooh, maybe some melon, blueberries. Here, let me give you some cash."

"Oh no, you can pay me later." Cheenah looked at the book on Lorna's kitchen table. "What is this?"

"This," Lorna picked it up, "is one of the new tenants! She's a published writer."

Cheenah reached for the book. "May I?"

"Of course."

She read the title, nodded her head, and murmured, "interesting," and turned the book over. "Oh, mi dios! She is most attractive."

Lorna said, "She's a wonderful writer. Why don't you take the book and read it? I think you'll fall in love with the story."

Cheenah nodded. "Yes, thank you. I would like that very much." She was still staring at the photograph of Mariella Vasquez, thinking, *maybe I will have to fall in love with the writer, too.*

SIX
October 7, 1980
Somewhere on Interstate 95 heading south

PK

PK rolled down the driver's side window even though it was raining. Her defroster worked part time, and she began to get that closed-in feeling again.

She hated freeway driving, and the tangle of highways around Maryland and Washington made her nervous, almost sick to her stomach.

She took in several deep gulps of air and tried to calm herself down. She wasn't even halfway to Florida yet.

She finally pulled off the highway after leaving the cities behind.

At the rest stop, she gratefully stretched and walked, paced really, around the welcome center. When she calmed down, she ordered some food from a deli vendor.

She felt so alone. Her last night in New York had been uneventful. Mel and the band bought her a few beers and tried to be upbeat, but because she had broken them up, there wasn't much to celebrate. Mel was cold and abrasive.

Jon had taken her out to dinner before the show and reiterated that he would wait patiently for her. "You're worth it," he'd said.

Her parents saw her briefly for dinner in the city the Sunday before she was to depart. "We hope you find what you're looking for," they'd said.

PK felt a dull ache in her chest as she drove away from the only life she had known up until now. When she crossed the state line into Pennsylvania out of New Jersey, she allowed her mind to drift. She knew she was making the right choice by leaving. It was time to close the chapter on her New York life.

PK's parents weren't happy that she'd chosen the rock lifestyle. They maintained that she was smart and could have a good career if only she applied herself.

But she *did* apply herself.

She bought her first guitar when she was in junior high school. She had saved all summer for it. It was a Gibson, and it sat in the window of Wegner's music store downtown. She stopped and stared at it every day and fantasized about having it on stage, impressing all the people who never thought she would amount to much in life.

As it turned out, she was a quick study and learned the basics in a matter of days. Her ear was keen. She could listen to a piece of music, pick out the chords and melodies, and re-create the sound on her guitar.

But her parents were sure it was just a phase.

PK knew differently.

She wrote songs from the dark parts of her heart; guitar riffs, melodies, and vocals.

But of late, the music and words seemed overdone. She felt like she had expended the gritty edge—and now, maybe a new opportunity to grow up and out of the immediate darkness was to be her path.

She was done with her family, had been for several years.

When she had answered the ad in the *Connection* and talked to Lorna Hughes in Florida, a light beckoned. A relief presented itself.

She crumpled up her sandwich wrapping, finished the rest of her cola, stopped at the rest room, and headed to the parking lot.

She said to herself as she climbed back into her old Datsun hatchback packed to the hilt with her equipment, "Maybe my life will be easier to navigate. I can do this."

The rain had stopped. The roads through Virginia presented PK with stunning vistas of rolling hills, rich verdant pastures of green against a sky where the thick storm clouds gave way to a brilliant blue.

She felt much better leaving the cities and clogged traffic behind. She donned her sunglasses and drove on with a new energy.

She started humming a tune. Something different. Something she would put guitar chords to when she put in for an overnight stay in Fayetteville. She figured if she could make it that far without stopping except for gas, food, and bathroom breaks, she would be halfway there.

More than halfway there.

SEVEN
October 7, 1980
Flight 5650 To Atlanta

LINDY

Lindy finally loosened the death grip on the armrests of her seat when the plane cleared the clouds after a bumpy ascent out of Chicago's O'Hare Airport. She wasn't fond of flying, but once things smoothed out, she was able to breathe normally.

A throaty female voice came over the loud-speaker system, "Good afternoon, ladies and gentlemen. The captain has turned off the fasten seat belt sign, and we will be starting our cabin service shortly. We ask you, while seated, to keep your seat belt loosely fastened in case we experience any unexpected rough air. The captain has stated that the weather looks smooth for our two-and-a half hour flight into the Atlanta airport, so, sit back, relax, and enjoy the flight!"

Lindy pushed her seat back to a more comfortable position and stole another glance at her seat partner, who had Walkman headphones on his head and his eyes closed.

She thought him lucky that he didn't seem to mind the whole ordeal of flying—the thrust of power as the big jet rumbled down the runway, the heady feeling of climbing quickly out of a city airport, the inevitable bumps and drops as the plane navigated in windy skies. It was exhilarating and physically taxing at the same time.

She preferred solid pavement underneath wheels *she* could control.

The clouds far below her window were white and puffy. The sky above her window expanded blue into a deeper blue offset by the sun to the east. She felt closer to her mother, closer to heaven's reach.

The flight was uneventful, the food was not bad, and when the plane landed in Atlanta it was seventy-eight degrees with a cloudless sky overhead. Lindy strode off the jetway and into her father's waiting arms at the gate.

"Daddy!" She cooed into his chest.

He hugged her close. "How's my girl?"

When they walked outside, Lindy took a deep breath and closed her eyes. The warm air felt so good on her city-paled skin. She put her face up to the sun. "Oh, how I've missed this."

Her father led them to the midnight-blue 1973 mint-condition convertible Mustang. "Well, here she is, all ready for you and your trip down to Florida! Do you want to drive her home?"

Lindy ran her hands along the smooth exterior, remembering how fabulous her mother looked driving the vehicle, with her scarf tied around her head and horn-rimmed sunglasses protecting her stunning green eyes from the sun, smiling big as she drove the eye-catching car around town. She would wave at neighbors and strangers alike, not a care in the world—just so damn happy in her midnight blue 'Stang.

Lindy's father tossed her the keys, "She's all yours, honey. Look in the glovebox. I brought mom's favorite kerchief for you to wear."

"Oh daddy. Thank you!" She pulled a red-and-white polka-dot scarf out of the glovebox, brought the fabric up to her nose and inhaled deeply, then tied it around her head.

She sighed and looked skyward before putting the car in reverse. *Just like you,* she thought with a slight lump in her throat. *Just like you, Mom.*

Lindy punched the gas pedal as she entered the expansive freeway system surrounding Atlanta. She felt her mother's energy all around her as she held the steering wheel in the ten-and-two position, just like mom, and relished the simplicity of the wind rushing around her face. Her heart filled with love, glad that her father sat next to her with a smile on his face.

Lindy thought it ironic that her parents, so loving, were separated by the cruelest of cruel in the form of cancer. They lived their lives unto themselves—without influence from society or familial expectations. They loved life, lived life, and gave freely of their goodwill.

Then the cancer shredded the picture, leaving Lindy, her father, and her siblings floating in neutral.

Ironic, because the adage *only the good die young* was so undeservedly true.

EIGHT
October 4, 1980
On the Road

Mariella stayed in a motel outside of Shreveport, Louisiana. She needed a shower and a real mattress to sleep on. The makeshift bed in the back of the van was getting old.

From her motel room, she called Barbara Grier at Naiad Press to inform her that she would be passing through.

Barbara was excited to see her and to discuss the new book proposal.

Marianna promised to share her work-in-progress, named, aptly, *Flawed.*

Naiad Press, based in Tallahassee, Florida, was founded by four women. When Barbara Grier first read the manuscript for *A Woman from Brazil*, in 1976, she shared it quickly with the other founders, and they all agreed to take Mariella on as a client.

Naiad spent the better part of a year editing, proofing, and shaping the book into a solid publication.

A reviewer out of Boston, who had gotten a complimentary copy of the book, read it in one sitting and went immediately to the New Words bookstore in Somerville, Massachusetts.

"You have to read this. Then carry it in your store. This will not disappoint. This will sell," the reviewer said pointedly.

The fire that started in Somerville spread quickly to the West Coast. In certain bookstores from Provincetown to San Francisco, *A Woman from Brazil* was situated up front in the window, with more books on a separate table.

The powers-that-be at Naiad were beyond ecstatic. Their already successful roster of writers, and the success of

Vasquez, made Naiad Press the frontrunner in the lesbian/feminist publishing field.

Mari was asked to do a book tour to meet and greet the women who had bought and read her book. Her contract stated that public appearances were a part of the deal, but when she got up in front of a crowd to read, her insides trembled. Because she couldn't breathe, her voice took on a squeaky quality, and it took away the impact of her words.

Barbara and the other founders of Naiad took her aside and coached her how to breathe and refocus to stay calm. It took some time, but eventually Mari was able to get through an appearance without throwing up either before or after and enjoy the reading.

She would think back to her college days, and how she knew she would write professionally, despite the public adoration. Her fans spent their money on her story. She was raised to pay forward kind gestures.

During her senior year at the University of New Mexico, she was invited to attend conference classes with established writers. Gloria Bretton-Tanner, a quirky but serious British author who published short stories, essays and four novels all after the age of fifty, was Mari's mentor.

In her lovely thick accent, Gloria oft intoned to her students, "While grammar is key in the final aspects of writing, the only thing to truly catch hold of the reader is to write from the *bones* of your soul."

Mariella kept that mantra in plain sight.

Write from the bones of your soul.

As she drove away from Shreveport, she finally felt good. The last day and a half had been fraught with an edgy anxiety; leaving her home, her parents back in Albuquerque—who were not pleased she was leaving New Mexico but understood she had to follow her path—and dear friends.

She was curious about The Pagoda Motel, and if the other artists in residence would be distracting.

But Lorna had assured her, vowing "quiet and remote."

Lorna explained that Heatherton County was a sleepy hamlet where people "just go about their business."

It sounded idyllic.

Maybe too idyllic?

Mari knew she was taking a big step by leaving her home and trying this new venture.

But it had been time to go.

And, as she drove, she felt a surge of excitement course through her veins.

A new journey, a new story.

Write from the bones of your soul.

NINE
October 9, 1980
Miami

DOREEN

Doreen turned the corner and drove into her uncle Vinnie's estate driveway in the affluent neighborhood of Coconut Grove. There was a gate and code box at the end of the apron.

The trip had been long, with lots of traffic from Fort Lauderdale all the way down to Miami, the early snowbirds repopulating the beach communities.

Milton whistled softly under his breath when he saw the estate.

Doreen nodded, "I know. The place is kind of huge."

Milton murmured, "Kind of? I think maybe *very* kind of."

Doreen keyed in the code. The huge wrought iron gate creaked open, giving way to a four hundred-foot, brick-paved driveway to the house. A tall stone fence surrounded the property and visibility was completely cut off from the road.

A voice squawked over the speaker attached to the gate pad.

"Doe? That you?"

"It's me, Vinnie. We're here."

"We?"

Doreen sighed, "Remember when I called you from the road, I told you I had Milton Catalvo with me? He's one of the caretakers at the motel."

Vinnie thought about it for a moment, "Oh yeah! Sure, I remember. He's gonna help you with your gear. Of course. Yeah, come on in!"

Milton's eyes were open wide. He shook his head and murmured, "Mama dios."

The House of Vinnie, as Doreen liked to call it, stood three stories high. Brick and mortar, arched entryways, and lots of foliage around the windows, which gave way to lush palm trees and various blooms around the perimeter of the house.

"Well, here we are."

Milton sat in his seat, turning his head this way and that, taking it all in. "This is all so very beautiful."

Doreen stepped out of the truck and stretched her back. "Wait till you see the backyard. The whole place, it's surrounded by stone walls. There's a pool and a Jacuzzi out back, too. Hope you brought your swim trunks."

Milton nodded, then made his way out of the truck. He was still mumbling when a man emerged from the front door and approached them.

"Doe! Let me see ya!"

Doreen smiled and hugged her uncle. He was thin, a bit pale, and his hair was mussed. She said into his bony shoulder, "How y'doin', Vin?"

"I have my good days and my not so good days. Today is one of those that could go either way."

Doreen turned to Milton. "Vin, this is Milton Catalvo."

Vinnie stretched out his hand and said, "Well, nice to meet yas. Come on in. Any friend of Doe's is a friend of mine. You two must be hungry and tired."

"Yeah, long drive but it was nice comin' down the coast."

Milton nodded, "So very nice to meet you, Uncle Vinnie."

Vinnie stopped for a moment then laughed, "Oh yeah! I can be *your* uncle, too."

Doreen took Milton by the elbow. "Come on, let's go inside where it's a bit cooler, and there's bound to be plenty of food and drink."

The inside of the house was cavernous. Marble floors, steps down into a sunken living room, arched doors leading off the foyer, large indoor plants, lots of windows.

Doreen headed straight for the kitchen. "This way."

Vinnie headed towards his home office. "I'll join yas in a few minutes, Doe. Was on the phone when you arrived, gotta make a call back."

Doreen nodded.

Betty Grable, the live-in "house manager" as Vinnie liked to call her, came running down the stairs.

She saw Doreen and called out, "There she is! My best girl!"

Doreen hugged her. "Ah gosh it's good to see you. You look great, Betty. Just great. Hey, this here is Milton Catalvo, one of the caretakers at the motel where I live. Milton, this is Betty Grable, but you can call her Betty. We named her that 'cause she looks like Betty Grable, the actress; you know of her?" Doreen wiggled her eyebrows and nodded towards her bustline.

Betty blushed but stood tall. "I am very proud of these, you know."

Milton's eyebrows were buried in his hairline. "Oh, so very nice to meet you, Miss Betty." His eyes fell to her bustline, and he tried hard, so hard to avert his stare.

This was not lost on Doreen. Betty was still attractive, but she was sharp and took no guff.

Betty said, "When y'gonna settle down and marry my son? He asks for you all the time. He's not gettin' any younger y'know."

Doreen put her hands upon Betty's shoulders, "You never give up, do you?"

Betty shrugged. "You still goin' round with the ladies?"

Doreen shook her head and started off to the kitchen. "Come on, Milton. Let's eat. I'm starved."

Milton shook Betty's hand and held on to it for a beat, then walked quickly to the kitchen with Doreen.

Later that evening, after a loud and slightly raucous dinner with the family, Doreen and Vinnie found themselves outside on the second-floor veranda, comfortably nestled in the deep-cushioned chairs, sipping after-dinner drinks, watching the sun lazily shift off towards the west, leaving an orange-blue sky accentuated by white drifting contrails from jet airplanes high above their heads.

Vinnie sipped his iced tea, and Doreen drank from a cold bottle of beer. He said, "You look good, Doe. Healthy. Not so skinny."

"I get well fed."

"So, tell me about this Loren gal, the one you mentioned at dinner."

Doreen took a long pull off the beer. "Her name is Lorna, and she's not a gal. She's a woman, through and through."

"So, tell me about this Lorna woman."

Doreen heard calypso music coming from down the street. The evening air was cool and warm at the same time, the night blooms spraying their scents out into the air and making the atmosphere heady and sweet. She put her head back on the chair and closed her eyes.

"She's a rock, Vin. A good, solid woman."

Vinnie remarked, "I was kinda hopin' the lady phase would peter out and you'd marry Betty's son. He asks about you all the time. I think you broke his heart."

"Oh, for Christ's sake I never had his heart. He's a lovesick puppy. I'm a lesbian, Vin. Through and through. Plus, the fact he damn near passes out every time I come into the room and I'm sure he's had his fair share of nighttime fantasies."

Vinnie put his glass down. "So, tell me. What are you going to do at this motel, the very motel your grandfather owned?"

"It's different now. The past is gone. Lorna has turned it into something solid, good, sincere, and real." She turned to face Vinnie. "I love her, Vinnie. Fair and square. I've never been in love before, but I know I'm in love now."

Vinnie nodded his head, still staring out at the darkening horizon. "So, tell me about your plans. I know you got something up your sleeve to come here with a U-Haul truck."

Doreen finished her beer. "I'm going to build a little garage of my own."

"Oh? Okay. You gonna do it on the motel property?"

"There's a half an acre next door to the motel, and the county doesn't want much for it, maybe five hundred. I asked if I could put a garage up—like a service station without the gas—and they told me it was zoned for residential. So, I explained it would be a garage. Like a residential garage. They finally told me I could build there, but it has to be built to town specs. A bunch of red tape."

Vinnie crossed his legs, cleared his throat, "Ah, that's nothin'. We could get around that. All we have to do is—"

"Vin, I'm going to do this myself. Milton and I talked about it on the way down here. He has cousins all over the place. We can get the cement poured and build the frame with help from his family."

"You don't want my help?"

Doreen turned to face him, "Just your blessing, really."

"What does Loren think about this?"

"Lorna. Lorna thinks it's a great idea. She's seen me in action. I've pretty much rebuilt Milton and Anya's van. Anya's pretty hard on equipment."

"Who d' hell is Enya?"

"AHnyah. She's Milton's wife. She's a firecracker, keeps us all in line. You'd like her, she's like Betty—a tough cookie who doesn't take shit from anyone."

"Yeah …" He leaned back in his chair and looked up at the stars with his arms behind his head. "So, what's with all the Mexicans, Doe? You turnin' tail on me? We got family, y'know."

"I know. But now they're my family, too."

"You were going to tell me about Lorna."

Doreen's heart skipped a beat. She missed her. She missed the dusty motel, the dunes, the sounds of the waves at night, and the salty air. "I'm pretty sure she's my soulmate. I can't imagine not being with her."

"Is she pretty?"

"Stunning, really. Dark hair, big green eyes, great body, killer smile."

"Sounds too good to be true. What's her angle?"

"Why does there always have to be an angle, Vin? She's a smart, educated, thoughtful, loving woman."

"Does she love ya? Treat you right?"

Doreen smiled, "Oh yeah. She treats me right."

"I think maybe I should meet this perfect woman sometime. If you love her like you say you do, then it has to be pretty serious."

"It is."

The calypso music from down the street dwindled out. A few shooting stars zipped across the sky.

Doreen's mind wandered.

They were sitting on top of a dune watching the horizon blue fade into a murky gray as the sun set to the west. The Peace Garden was beginning to look like a garden, but they still had quite a bit of work to do.

A few stars blinked to life as the sun continued to set.

Lorna had brought a picnic basket of cheese, bread, wine, and cold cuts down to the beach. Doreen laid out a blanket for them and they sat, arms touching, watching the peacefully receding day slip into a sultry night sky.

"I like it here, Lorna. It's so different."

"How so?"

"Well, for one thing, you're here."

Lorna smiled out towards the ocean. "I'm listening."

"And, well, I feel like I can be myself. Like, I don't have to always be on guard. Anya and Milton, and Cheen are like family. Everyone seems so ... I dunno ... at peace with themselves, know what I mean?"

Lorna took Doreen's arm in her palm. "I do. And you blend in quite well."

"I want to get to know you, Lorna. And I want you to get to know me. I've never felt that with anyone else. I'm usually runnin' by now or fucking things up. Relationships are not my strong suit." She cleared her throat. "But you're different, Lorn."

Lorna laid her head on Doreen's shoulder. "You are too. I like having you here. I like seeing you out in the garden with Milton and his boys. I like seeing you across from me at a table in a restaurant. Or coming up the stairs to my bedroom. I like being on the back of your bike, holding on to you. You're solid."

Doreen leaned down and kissed Lorna on the forehead. "I'd like to think I could stay for a while?"

"I'd like to think that too." Lorna reached up and took Doreen's face in her hands. She lightly kissed her nose, her cheeks, and her third eye. "I think I'd like that so very much."

Vinnie's voice brought Doreen back to the present. "If you need any help, Doe, Frank Salucci and his boys are up there in Jacksonville." He sighed deeply. "But ... I know you'll do okay. You always land on your feet. You were the smart one. Your brother, the big-shot artist with no future. Your mother, she's got a big heart but y'know, she's a few cans shy of a six in the brains department. Your father knew you'd go places."

Doreen chuckled, "I have. I've put almost 30,000 miles on that bike."

"Yeah, what a bike that is. You did good, Doe. Real good."

"And that's another reason I want my tools and gear. I gotta keep the bike in good runnin' shape. I gotta get new tires, and she might need a new carb."

Vinnie yawned, "I can get you the parts you need. Just lemme know, and I'll have 'em for you before you leave."

Doreen sat up and stretched. "Thanks Vin. That help I'll take."

Vinnie stood up and wobbled. "Ahhh, it's time for me to turn in."

Doreen stood up and took hold of his arm to walk him into the house. "How are you, really?"

Vinnie took a minute to get his legs underneath him. "Not so hot, Doe. This liver thing really kicked my ass to China. Seems like a bunch more parts are startin' to fall apart. My bowels are always gassy, my heart flutters all over the place, and my dick lives in the next county."

Doreen held on to him a little tighter. "I don't like it, Vin. Have you seen the doc?"

Vinnie snorted and cocked his head, "Ach, what d'hell do *they* know." They walked a bit in silence. Doreen led him into the house and down the hall to his bedroom.

She asked, "The boys keeping their noses clean?"

"Ah, yeah. They're fine. They watch me like a hawk; so does BettyGrable. It's like she's invisible until I do something stupid, and then she materializes outta thin air."

Doreen chuckled. "That's why she's still here. You can't live without her."

"No." Vinnie stopped at his door. "I can't." He looked her square in the eye. "I'm glad you're settlin' down, Doe. I'm glad you're not like Georgie. He's so ... scattered."

"When's he out for parole?"

"Ach, maybe in three months."

"Is he comin to live with you?"

"Naw. He's got some dame in Miami."

"Well, don't' tell him where I live."

"I won't."

After getting Vinnie settled in for the night, Doreen found Milton at the pool, snoring away on a lounge chair. He had a big soft towel around his legs. Doreen pulled it up to cover his torso. He shifted, opened one eye, and fell back to sleep.

She went into the house to the guest wing, shut the door behind her, and picked up the phone. Doreen dialed Lorna's private line. It rang several times before Lorna answered. Doreen almost hung up.

"Hey you!" Lorna was out of breath.

"What? Did you just run the fifty-yard dash?"

"Almost. The first tenant, PK, arrived about fifteen minutes ago, and I was just giving her the tour of the compound."

"Sounds fantastic. And what about the others?"

"I haven't heard from Alice or Mari. I assume they are en route. But Lindy called me this morning and said she was leaving Atlanta later this afternoon, would probably stop overnight somewhere. So, tell me, how was your trip down? How is Vinnie?"

"Well, Vinnie isn't doing so hot. He looks like shit, really. I mean, he's still got his mind and all, but his body looks like he's been dragged from one end of the beach to the other. He tells me things are failing left and right."

"I'm sorry, honey."

"Yeah, it's weird to see him like that." Doreen leaned back on the headboard of the bed in the guest room. "The drive down was good though. Lots of traffic, snowbirds descending as usual. Milton almost fell out of the truck when he saw the House of Vinnie."

Lorna laughed. "The House of Vinnie. Sounds like a good name for a sitcom."

Doreen absently looked around at the slightly garish but well-appointed decorations in the guest suite. She said, "I miss you."

Lorna softened. "I miss you too. It's not quite the same without you here. When do you think you'll head back this way?"

"Couple of days. Vinnie has to get some parts for me, and I have to pack boxes."

"All the renters should be here by the time you get back."

"Did you see the moon tonight?" Doreen closed her eyes.

"Yes, it's stunning. Almost full. The only thing missing is you."

"I know. It's not the same."

"You sound tired, honey."

"Yeah, I'm pretty beat from the drive. Let's talk tomorrow then?"

Lorna purred, "Will you call me when you wake up?"

"You'll be the first call I make."

They bid each other goodnight and rang off.

Doreen sat for a moment on the bed. An odd silence surrounded her. She was very aware of her heartbeat, of the blood pulsing through her body. The essence of Lorna's voice drifted in and out of her ears.

She sighed and tried to reason why she felt a little unsure of things. Why Lorna's quick shift in focus from her to the arrival of the new tenants at this moment bothered her.

She muttered, "No shit, Shirl. You're not the only woman there now."

She had been the focus of Lorna's attentions for the last several months, and now the renters were arriving. Things would change.

A flutter of insecurity swept through her gut. What if one of the women was more attractive to Lorna than she was? More educated, more talented?

"Of course, they are, Doe." She murmured into the large room. "They have degrees, they went to college, and they're talented."

Doreen shook her head and made herself get up to do her ablutions before retiring for the night.

In the bathroom mirror, she regarded herself. She knew she was good-looking, in excellent shape, and had several talents of her own, even if college was never in her game plan.

It was just this nagging voice that said she wasn't in the same league as Lorna and her ilk. That she was less-than, a mafia kid. A woman who lived off the proceeds of dark dealings, swindles, and fast ones. Of connections with people who thought nothing of killing someone else face-to-face. Or using the family honor card like a shield or a sword to justify the senseless killings.

It was murder she never understood. When she witnessed her father die by two bullets, she couldn't fathom how those two small pieces of metal could bring a person down, *forever*. And why?

She sat down hard on the commode and put her head in her hands. She felt her throat constrict, her heart thud. She grabbed a nearby towel and let her pain pour out into the folds.

She was not good at being vulnerable.

To make matters worse, at that moment an old tape replayed clearly in her mind. The words spoken to her by a woman she'd jilted shortly before meeting Lorna.

"What the hell, Doreen? All you seem to do is run from one city to the next on that fucking bike of yours, breaking hearts along the way. When are you going to stop running? When are you going to admit that you've got to stop long enough to *unfuck* the damage you suffered as a kid? It's not going to go away on its own. Karma will follow you; you know that, right? I mean, you just keep taking it with you wherever you go and one day ..."

Doreen remembered walking out the door after that speech with all those words stuck to her as if she were covered in glue. Words that propelled her towards the bike, toward the wind, toward the only freedom she knew. Away from another heart she made promises to, knowing she could not keep them.

She dried her tears with the towel, grabbed a tissue and blew her nose, sighed, stood up, grabbed her kit, and pulled out a toothbrush and paste.

"Knock it off." She spat the paste into the sink. "Just knock it off. You're going to prove them *all* wrong."

She gargled with mouthwash and smacked her lips. "That's better."

Doreen turned off the lights in the bathroom, dimmed the lights in the bedroom, and pulled back the sheets.

A slight knock came at her door.

She opened it to find Milton standing there with the towel wrapped around his torso. "So very sorry to disturb you, Miss, but I think I got lost to find my room. I know it is down this hall somewhere."

Doreen smiled at him. She felt a huge wave of relief wash over her. Milton represented the connection to the motel, to the life that she found herself willingly and happily committed to.

She said, "Follow me. Hey, are you hungry by chance?"

He shrugged his shoulders, "I am never one to turn down the possibility of good food."

"Let's hit the fridge."

"Oh yes, Miss. Is this towel okay to go to the fridge?"

Doreen smiled at him. "Milton, you are, in my book, okay to go anywhere in whatever you choose to wear."

He shrugged his shoulders and followed her down the hall to the grand staircase.

TEN
The Pagoda Motel

It was mid-afternoon on a sultry fall day when Mariella pulled into the turnaround in front of the main building. Her first view of the property was the Peace Garden.

She got out of her car and walked toward it, the scents of the blooms and colors reminding her of her beloved desert garden.

She breathed deep through her nose. "So lush," she murmured.

"Hello?" A voice called out from behind.

She turned to see Lorna walking towards her with an extended hand. "You must be Mariella. I'm Lorna."

Mariella shook her hand. "It's so nice to meet you. This garden, the photographs did not do it justice at all. It is so very beautiful. Did you get my check? And the book?"

Lorna smiled, "Thank you. And yes, I received both. Your book is magnificent."

Mariella blushed, "You read it already? Well, wow. Thank you!"

Lorna said, "I read it in one night. I couldn't put it down. You and I, well, Julianna and I, have a lot in common!"

"Really? We must talk then!"

"Come, you must be tired from your drive. Would you like to stop into the lobby for refreshment? I have some paperwork for you to fill out along with a welcome package and so on. Or would you rather go directly to your cabin and we can deal with the paperwork later?"

"I could use a bathroom and something cold to drink."

Lorna took her gently by the shoulder and directed her to the front door of the lobby. "I just happen to have both."

Lorna felt like a schoolgirl meeting a crush. Not a sexual

crush, more like admiration.

Lorna's first impression of Mariella was that Mariella was genuine. Maybe a little nervous, but real. She was quiet, direct. Kept eye contact and waited for responses.

If anyone was nervous, it was Lorna.

***

A few weeks later, Lorna sat down to write a letter to Avril.

```
Hello dear:                    October 25

Just thought I'd drop you a line since you
and Saul are in Jalisco Bay and we will miss
our biweekly chat. I hope the two of you had
a wonderful vacation (without the kiddos!).

Life here at the motel is pretty darn good.
All the tenants are in; they seem to be
settling nicely. Mariella was the last one to
arrive—she had spent some time in Tallahassee
with her publisher. Did you have a chance to
find the book in Cleveland? Last we talked
you hadn't been able to find it. Check
Coventry Books. They can order it for you if
they don't have it on the shelf. I don't know
why I didn't think of that first off.

So, for two Tuesdays in a row, we've all
gotten together and had dinner at El Mocambo.
The whole gang—Anya and Milton, Cheenah, and
the tenants. I think it's going to be a
regular thing now! Then afterwards we head
back to the beach to build a bonfire. It's a
great way to connect with the tenants without
getting in their way.

They're all so different, unique. Like, PK—
the musician—she's so focused on her music. I
can hear her at different times of the day. I
like her voice and the way she plays the
guitar (especially after reading Mariella's
```

book).

And Lindy—the graphic artist. She's a riot. It took me a little while to get comfortable with her. She's quite assertive. LOVES to talk. She's got that Southern accent, and way with words that makes her sound like she's reading from a script for a play. She drove up to the motel in a gorgeous midnight blue convertible Mustang. Doreen almost tripped over herself to look underneath the hood.

And Alice—the artist—is just plain funky. It's the best way to describe her. She's always got paint stains on her hands and clothes. The other day she was outside of her cabin in a skinny-ribbed undershirt and gym shorts stretching her canvases to different sized frames. I didn't realize how incredibly thin and pale she is. We've got to fatten her up and get her face to the sun!

And of course, there is Mariella. She is such a lovely woman, Avril. She is older than the rest, just turned forty. I feel like I can relate to her better than the others because we are closer in age. Sometimes, when I look at her while the group is together, she is somewhere else. I don't mean to say she is vacant and doesn't participate. She takes it all in. Maybe stows it somewhere for later use? I think the other ladies look up to her. She's well balanced. AND guess who has eyes for her? Cheenah! I gave her my copy of Mariella's book and she read it in one sitting, like I did. She was starry eyed when she returned the book. It's sweet to see her all flustered around Mariella.

Doreen's garage is going swimmingly. She and Milton work out there all day. Did I tell you Alice is designing a mural on the side of the garage for Doreen? I saw a preliminary sketch

```
and it's so freakin' cool. I'll take pictures
when it's done.

Well, it's Tuesday and we are heading across
the intracoastal for dinner in about twenty
minutes. The weather is stellar, so we're
going to do the bonfire thing.

I miss you. Hugs to Saul and the kids.
Talk soon.
Love

L-
```

Lorna sealed and stamped the envelope and put it with the rest of the outgoing mail, then got ready for the Tuesday Taco feast at El Mocambo.

***

Lorna, Doreen, Alice, and Lindy were left to watch the embers of the fire crackle down to a small orange glow. Mariella had gone back to her cabin to write, PK was tired, and Cheenah had gone back to work directly after dinner.

Doreen asked Alice, "So, how did you get the nickname Lucky?"

Alice had been sketching mindlessly in the semi-darkness. She closed her sketchpad. "My sister."

Lorna said, "Oh, older or younger?"

"Um, younger. She passed away recently."

A silence befell the group.

"Oh, my God. I am so sorry, Alice." Lorna gently said.

Alice brought her knees up to her chest and stared into the fire. "She died six months ago."

Lindy asked quietly, "Was she ill?"

"She was born with Down Syndrome, but she also had heart issues. She was eight years younger than me." She took in a deep breath, let it out, then continued. "See, Alice is really my middle name. My *first* name is Lucille. But Cora, that was my sister, couldn't pronounce it so it came out as Lucky. To Cora, I was always Lucky. So it stuck." She shifted her body to sit cross-legged. "Cora wanted to learn how to draw, so before I left for college, I taught her about colors and such. She had problems with space and dimension and point-of-view, but she loved to color and paint. Her stuff was cool, kind of like Dali. Rudimentary and without rules. She loved to come down to the pier and paint with me. It was our special time." Alice bowed her head, tears collecting on her face.

Doreen said gently, "I'd have to say she was pretty lucky herself to have a sister like you."

Alice sniffed and tossed a few small pieces of driftwood into the fire. "Yeah."

Lorna asked, "So, was coming down here hard for you? To leave your parents and home?"

Alice shook her head. "No. It was a light in the tunnel. After Cora passed, I came to a complete standstill creatively. I couldn't even be in the house. Cora's spirit was everywhere. My parents were beside themselves. The three of us couldn't even talk to one another. Cora's passing left a hole in our lives. I was aimless. Then your ad came up in the *Connection*, and I was sure some …" She flailed her hand toward the sky. "Some higher power put it there. For me, anyhow."

Lorna put her hand on Alice's knee. "This is a safe place, Alice."

Lindy said, "My mother died four years ago, and … and … there is still a big old empty space in my family, too."

"My God! I'm so sorry." Lorna shook her head, adding quietly, "My father died late last year."

Alice sifted sand through her hands.

Lindy said softly, "I am sorry, Lorna and Alice. You know, the years do not take away the pain. They just make it easier to contend with. Sometimes, anyhow."

Doreen added, "Well, my father died when I was fifteen."

They all looked at one another, then away at the dark ocean.

Doreen put two more logs on the fire, stirred it up with a longer stick, and said, "I think another round is calling. Don't you ladies think so?" She stood up and said, "I'll be right back. I happen to have a six-pack cooling in my fridge." She kissed Lorna on the lips and headed off the beach.

Lorna watched her recede into the night, the moon showing only a quarter light. She found herself thinking of her father, as well as Lindy's mom and Alice's sister and Doreen's dad. She thought it was interesting that the four of them decided to remain on the beach after the others left.

When she turned back to face Alice and Lindy, Lindy was smiling. She said, "I like your woman, Lorna. She's top-notch and, if you will, quite hot in the looks department. Those eyes ..." Lindy did not reveal that she had a major crush on her.

"Thank you, I rather like them myself." Lorna noticed Lindy staring at the now empty trail up to the motel.

Doreen jogged back to the fire area and put the six pack on top of the cooler. "Who's ready?"

As they all grabbed a cold one, Doreen settled back down next to Lorna.

Alice said, "You know when Cora died, it didn't seem real. I mean, we all knew she was going downhill quickly, but it just didn't seem real, especially when we came home from the hospital on the night she died, without her. Nothing felt right."

Lindy set her beer can down in the sand. "I know. When my mother died—stage four ovarian that they didn't catch in time—we knew. We were prepared. It was a slow awful drag downhill. Well, we *thought* we were prepared. She died at home you see." She took in a deep breath. "We were all around her, twenty-four seven, taking turns at her side. She was never alone. When she took her last breath and the mortician came to take her away, there was this ... this cavernous space, the empty hospital bed. It was like it didn't belong in the house. We were all lost for so long, my brother, sister, dad and me. Just lost."

Lorna nodded. "Just awful. I'm so sorry." She dug her toes deeper into the cool sand. "My father and I really didn't see eye to eye until I graduated law school. I wished it hadn't been that way, that we'd had the chance to get to know one another. Or rather, he had had the chance to get to know me. He was so healthy. He went so fast."

Alice asked, "Heart attack?"

"Yeah. Right in the middle of a board meeting." She snorted lightly. "They, the medical community, called it the widow-maker. Some strange anomaly he was born with. Hidden in the deep dark depths of the heart. He just ... went." Lorna rested her chin on her drawn-up knees.

Alice asked Doreen, "How did your dad die? Heart attack, too?"

Doreen looked at Lorna and slowly nodded her head. "You could say that."

The group was silent, lost in their own private heartache. Lorna stroked Doreen's face in the dimming light of the fire.

Alice sighed, stood up, and brushed off her jeans. "Well, I think it's time for me to turn in."

Lindy followed suit. "Me, too."

Lorna said, "I hope you guys sleep well."

Lorna and Doreen waited until Alice and Lindy disappeared down the path.

Lorna took a stick and shoved the embers around. "I wonder what everyone is going to do for Thanksgiving." She turned and looked at Doreen over her shoulder. "Do you usually spend the time with Vinnie and his boys?"

Doreen sighed. "Ach, I dunno this year. Last year I was at Bambi's in Atlanta, and she had her usual cast of misfits over. It was all right but going to Vinnie's is more fun."

"Bambi?"

"My mother."

Lorna raised an eyebrow. "You call your mother Bambi?"

Doreen chuckled, "Yeah, she always looks like a deer in the headlights. Especially since she decided to have surgery on her eyelids. They were drooping."

Lorna laughed, "Oh my God."

"What about you? You thinkin' of headin' up to

Cleveland? See Avril and your mom and brothers and such?"

"I don't know either. I kind of want to stay down here with the family. Anya explained that they do a big feast over at Anita and Luis's house. It sounds like fun. Cleveland is usually such a formal affair. And now with my dad gone ..."

"Sure, I get it. Come here." Doreen opened her arms.

Lorna situated herself so she could still feel the warmth of the fire but be close to Doreen. "Maybe we should open up the lobby and kitchen for the people who want to stay here," she said. "Maybe have Anita and Luis and the family here instead."

"Sounds like a good idea. I think it would be fun. I'm not real interested in going to Atlanta, truth be known."

Lorna snuggled in closer. "Let's make some traditions here right here this year."

Doreen held Lorna tighter. "What say you we make some history right now on this beach?"

Lorna climbed on top of Doreen and kissed her. "Great minds ..."

ELEVEN
That Same Night

Lindy tossed and turned and finally flicked on the clamp lamp attached to her drafting table. The clock on the nightstand said 3:22.

"Crap." She muttered as she made her way to the bathroom.

After relieving herself, she went to the little fridge and pulled out a jug of water. She was dehydrated with the remnant tastes of spicy Mexican food and beer lingering in her mouth.

She quietly opened her screen door and sat down on the top step, sipping the cold water slowly so she wouldn't get a headache. The night air was peaceful. The nocturnal animals chatted with one another, and insects fluttered around.

She couldn't stop thinking of her mother. After the conversation at the bonfire her heart became heavy. For some reason her new surroundings reminded her of Vera every day. Once she thought she smelled Vera's unique perfume while walking towards the lobby.

Lindy stood up and decided to walk down to the beach. She needed a good cry. There was something cathartic about crying with saltwater so close by.

When she got to the water's edge, she took off her flip-flops.

Suddenly, something latched itself on to her pinky toe and she screamed out loud.

"Ow, oh my God! What the hell—?" she shook her foot and backed up from the water. "Get the hell off my foot!" She jumped all over the place, eventually losing her balance and landing on her rear end.

A voice came from behind her. "Hey, what's going on? Is everything all right?"

Lindy called out, "No! There's something biting the hell out of my toe!"

Alice approached Lindy. "Okay, hang on. Let me see if I can tell what it is. Hold still."

Lindy cried out, "Well, whatever it is, it won't let go!"

Alice reached down and grabbed Lindy's foot. "Hang on, I think it's a ... hang on, try to hold still. I think I've got it."

Lindy screeched, "Oh my God! What is it?" She was starting to panic. Pain rushed up her leg and into her groin. "Get it off!"

"It's off."

Her foot burned. "What was it?" Her breath was ragged.

Alice chuckled and tried to show Lindy what it was in the dark. All Lindy could see was something small dangling from Alice's fingers. A little claw.

Lindy sat up, "Jeez, what the hell?"

"A little crab." Alice tossed the freaked-out critter back into the water.

Lindy tried to steady her breathing while rubbing her foot. Her pinky toe felt broken. Her calf ached.

Alice said, "Can you stand up?"

"I think so. Can you give me a hand?"

Alice helped Lindy up, but Lindy could barely apply pressure to the foot. Lindy held onto Alice's shoulder for support. "Thanks. I don't know what I would have done if you weren't here."

Lindy tried to put her weight on her foot. It was touch and go for a moment, but as the pain subsided she was able to bear weight. "And what are *you* doing down here anyhow?"

Alice helped Lindy walk. "I could ask the same."

They walked in silence for a few moments until Alice asked, "So, what *are* you doing down here?"

"I couldn't sleep. You?"

"Yeah, couldn't sleep."

They walked again in silence; then Lindy said, "I think the conversation at the bonfire was tough."

"Yes, very hard."

Lindy looked at Alice in the dark. "You doing all right? You wanna talk?"

Alice sighed. "I feel so lost."

Lindy kept her arm around Alice's shoulders. "I know, honey. I get it."

Alice stifled a sob.

"It's okay. Go ahead," Lindy said. "It's the reason I came down here just now. I needed a cry, and I didn't want to wake anyone up in the compound. And then all my screaming. I'm surprised we don't see flashlights bobbing on the path down here."

Alice started to laugh instead of cry.

"What?" Lindy cocked her head and looked at Alice.

Alice said, "You, jumping around."

"Wha ... you're *laughing* at—" Lindy started to chuckle because Alice's laughter was so contagious.

Alice could barely get the words out because she was laughing so hard. "I wish I could have videotaped you because ..." she cackled and bent over, "it was just so dang unexpected and fuckin' hysterical! I mean, here I am feeling like shit—" she cackled some more, "and then *you* come along and start screaming like a girl and hopping around and—" Alice fell onto the sand, holding her gut.

Lindy plopped down next to her. "Oh, my Gawd. I must have looked like a complete spazz!"

The two of them giggled into the quiet night, and after a while, they toned it down.

Alice said, "Holy shit that was funny. I mean, not *funny* in that you were in pain, but if you could have seen what I saw while I was crying my eyes out."

Lindy caught her breath. "Well, didn't Joni Mitchell sing something about laughing and crying was the same release?"

"She did."

"Man, look at those stars."

Alice rolled onto her back. "Yeah. Sometimes I look for Cora in the stars, like maybe she's up there hanging out, watching over me."

"She might just be."

Alice sighed. "Oh, what I wouldn't give to see her right now."

Lindy sighed too. "I know." She called out toward the sky, "Vera, where are you?"

"Vera was your mom?"

"Yeah."

Alice leaned up on one elbow, facing Lindy. She bent down and kissed Lindy on the lips.

Lindy drew back, "Wait, *whaa*?"

Alice put her fingers up to Lindy's lips. "Shhh. Close those beautiful eyes and just go with it."

"But—"

Alice silenced her with another kiss.

TWELVE
November 24, 1980

Lorna sat at her desk in the office behind reception doing her bills when she heard the front door open. She listened for a moment, then stood up and entered the lobby. When she saw who stood at the threshold of the door, she froze.

"*Mother?*" she gasped.

"So, *this* is where you've been hiding?" With the sun behind her, Esther resembled a Rubenesque silhouette.

Lorna couldn't speak.

"Well, aren't you going to invite me in?" Her strong hefty voice rang out.

Lorna shook herself out of her state. "Of course! Come in, mother, come in." She moved forward and came around the desk. "How did you ... why didn't you call? I would have—"

Esther strode into the lobby and looked around, waving Lorna off. "Isn't this just quaint?" she remarked. She touched the furniture as she walked by, looking at the stereo, television console, and the front desk. "Look at *this*! How lovely!"

"Mother, why didn't you call? I would have picked you up at the airport, prepared the guest room."

Esther asked, "*Who* did this woodwork?"

Lorna went up to her. "Mother!"

"What? Oh."

Lorna went to hug her. "I'm just so shocked to see you."

Esther hugged her daughter with one arm and only for a moment. "Well, your brothers are busy for Thanksgiving. We are doing Christmas together, which I hope you'll join us for, at the house. I've had several invitations from people, but I thought I would come down here and see if you wanted to have dinner with me."

Lorna thought about the Thanksgiving plans she had made with everyone. She was going to host a potluck at the motel since her tenants were not going to go home for the holiday. Lindy's father was invited, due to arrive tomorrow.

She said, "Well, of course you're welcome here but I am hosting a potluck dinner …"

Her mother looked at her, waiting for her to finish her sentence. "And?"

"Where is your luggage? You'll want to change out of that suit and into something more breezy. It's unusually warm today."

Her mother's suit—lightweight linen—looked as crisp as if she had just donned it. Lorna could never understand how her mother could pull things off like that after a long flight and drive.

"In the trunk of the rental car." Esther handed Lorna the keys to the car and surveyed the rest of the lobby. "So very quaint."

Lorna ran out, grabbed her mother's belongings, and zipped back into the lobby. "The guest room is upstairs. It's small, though. Are you sure you don't want me to book you a room on the mainland?"

"Oh nooo! I'm fine, really."

"Well, I haven't had the chance to dust up there. The last time someone was in it was months ago when Avril came down for a visit."

"Oh? How is the dear girl?"

Lorna was still wondering how all this happened. Small talk was the last thing she could muster. She led her mother up the steep steps to the guest room.

"Well, here you—"

Esther exclaimed, "Pink! How delightful! Such a cute room, Lorna. A bit small, but I think I can manage."

Lorna pulled a portable luggage rack out of the hall closet and set her mother's suitcase on it. "I know, that's why I thought you'd be more comfortable at a motel on the—"

"Babe?" A voice called from downstairs, "you in here, honey?"

Lorna stood stock-still with her back to her mother. She could sense Esther's eyebrows rise.

"Um. Upstairs," she called out weakly.

"Honey, can you give me a hand with something. I've got grease all over the place, and I—"

"I'll be right down." Lorna called out. She turned to face her mother but could not look her in the eye.

Esther said quietly, "Go ahead. I'll just unpack and freshen up a bit."

Lorna took in a very deep breath, nodded slightly, and bolted down the steps.

When she saw Doreen, she ushered her quickly to the kitchen and then outside through the back door.

"What the—," Doreen said.

"My *mother* just showed up!" Lorna hissed.

"*What*? No fuckin' way!" Doreen hissed back.

They were outside behind the main building. Lorna paced. They kept their voices low.

"Didn't she call or anything?" Doreen watched Lorna make tracks in the hard-packed dirt and sand.

"No! She didn't call! I had no idea!"

"What are you going to do?"

"What *can* I do? She's my mother for God's sake!"

"But she doesn't know about—"

"I *know*!"

Lorna continued to pace with her arms across her chest. She had to *think*. "I have to figure this out before things get out of hand." She paced and then looked at Doreen, "What did you need?"

Doreen took a rag out of her back pocket and wiped at her hands. "Don't worry about it, hon. I'll go find Milton."

"They're out getting supplies for the dinner."

"Oh shit, that's right. Thanksgiving."

Lorna shuddered.

"Oh, Lorn. What can I do?"

"Just give me a minute to think things out. I mean, I can't very well hide everything from her."

Doreen shook her head. "If you need me, holler. Sorry I

spilled the beans. I didn't know anyone was here."

"No, it's okay. It was bound to come out some time. I just didn't think it would be now."

Doreen blew her a kiss and walked back to her garage.

Lorna went back into the main building via the back door, her nerves on edge.

Trying to hide her discomfort she called up the stairs in a more jovial voice than she felt. "Mother? Can I bring you a cold drink? Iced tea or lemonade?"

Her mother answered flatly, "Iced tea would be lovely, Lorna. Thank you."

Lorna fussed in the kitchen trying to buy some time. Maybe if she just ignored the endearments from Doreen, the ones her mother heard clear as day, they could carry on as if nothing had happened.

Lorna filled a glass with ice and poured the fresh-brewed tea. She cut a lemon into wedges and found a straw in the cupboard.

She climbed the steps, praying for a sudden tornado.

"Here you are." Lorna did not meet her mother's eye as she handed her the iced tea. "I'm sorry I didn't get a chance to dust. Here, let me get this done quickly." She went into the hall closet, pulled out a rag and a spray can of furniture polish and said lightly, "This won't take but a moment."

Her mother stepped aside and sipped her beverage.

Lorna continued to talk. "So, how is the house? Norman and Gail?"

"Fine."

Lorna dusted over the same area twice. Her mother returned to her unpacking. Or more like rearranging the contents of her suitcase.

"Lorna?" Esther said with her back to her daughter.

Lorna could feel it coming. Her throat threatened to close. She continued dusting. "Yes?"

Her mother turned slightly, "Do you have something you want to tell me?"

Lorna froze in place. *No, this cannot be happening right now. I'm not—*

Esther now turned to face her daughter head on. "Well,

do you?"

Lorna thought for a moment that she might vomit. Why couldn't her mother have just stayed in Cleveland, where the distance between them kept everything in stasis, where she did not have to admit to her lifestyle?

"What do you think I need to tell you, Mother?" Lorna picked up the dusting again.

"Do I make you uncomfortable?"

"Your unexpected arrival has me a bit rattled."

"They say the element of surprise is the best way to reveal the truth."

"Is that why you came down here?" Dusting furiously now.

"Well, partially. With your father gone I've had a lot of time to think and mull things over. I know that you and I haven't seen eye to eye, but I think it's time to forge ahead, don't you think, Lorna?"

Lorna had stowed the rag and polish in the hall closet while her mother said this. She closed the closet door slowly and stood at the threshold of the room, her arms across her chest. "What is it you want to know, Mother?"

"I think you know."

Lorna breathed deep and let it out. "Fine."

Another silence.

"Lorna?"

"Yes, Mother, I am a lesbian."

Her mother smirked and nodded her head. "How long have you been … this way, Lorna?"

"Most of my life."

"So, the boyfriends in high school and college were smoke screens for our benefit?"

"Yes."

"Why did you have to lie about it?"

Lorna felt her temperature rise. "I don't want to seem ungracious, Mother, but it was hard being who I really was growing up."

"You were a very happy young lady, Lorna. You excelled in all your studies, you had oodles of friends, you—"

Lorna cut in. "I had to live two lives, Mother."

"Hmph. Well, I didn't see that coming." She turned back to her suitcase. "And why did you feel you had to do that?"

"Mother …"

"And that girl, Jeanette?"

"Do you mean Jeanie?"

"Yes."

"She was my first love."

"Well, it all makes sense now." Esther took her clothes out of the suitcase and put them on the bed. "And the woman who spoke the endearments just a little while ago. Who is she?"

"Doreen. She is my lover."

"Well," Esther sighed. "I'm not entirely surprised by your admission but it's going to take some getting used to. I'll tell you that your father and I had discussions about this, and I respect you for keeping it quiet, what with your father's very public business affiliations and possible run for governor."

"Yes, mother."

"Is that why you moved so far away?" She turned to look at her daughter.

"Partially. After Dad died, I realized that I didn't have to live in his shadow anymore."

Esther shook her head. "Your father was very proud of you. I'm sorry you felt you had to live in his shadow." This was said with a tinge of sarcasm.

"What can I say, Mother? You came down here to get the truth and now …" Lorna looked down at her painted toenails. She saw a little chip on the right great toe.

The front door to the main building banged open. "Hola?"

Lorna called out, thanking God silently for the interruption. "Upstairs. Be right down."

Esther whispered, "Who is that?"

"My caretakers. Why don't we go downstairs so you can meet them?" Lorna was already heading down the steps. She heard her mother follow.

"Hello, Miss Lorna, we got the—oh! You have some

company?"

Lorna said, "Anya, Milton. This is my mother, Esther."

Anya dropped two of the bags she carried in on the floor next to her. "Oh! So nice to meet you, Miss Easter!"

Esther extended her hand, "Well, it's Esther, no 'e-a.'"

"Of course. Miss Ester. I am Anya Catalvo and this is my husband, Milton."

"So nice to meet you, Enya."

"Yes, well, it is *Anya,* no 'eyn.'"

Lorna groaned.

Milton shook Esther's hand in both of his. "So very nice to meet you, Miss Ester."

"Caretakers! How wonderful."

Anya said excitedly, "Miss Lorna, you did not say anything about Miss Ester coming for Thanksgiving!"

Lorna's eyes widened. She did not have an opportunity to signal to Anya to zip it without her mother seeing the gesture.

Anya continued. "You will be staying for Thanksgiving, Miss Ester? We will have a big crowd and so much great food."

Esther smiled. "Why, how lovely!" She looked at her daughter. "I wouldn't miss it for the world." She then turned back to Anya. "Will you need anything? Can I pick up dessert or appetizers?"

Lorna stepped in, "Well, the food is pretty well planned out and—"

Anya cut her off. "Maybe more pies?" She looked at Milton. He shrugged. "Hokay, pies will be the best, I think. Donchu think, Miss Lorna?"

Lorna lost the battle. "Sure." This meant that her mother was staying. For Thanksgiving.

"Well, Mother?"

"It's the least I can do for surprising you."

Anya's smile faded. "Oh!" She caught on and looked at Lorna, who returned the look with a deep sigh. "A surprise! Well then. Milton and I will unpack the van. We have much to do."

When Anya and Milton went quickly into the kitchen with the first load of bags, Lorna turned to her face her mother. "Well, while we're on this unexpected but necessary truth adventure, I supposed it's time to tell you what goes on around here."

"Shall we take a walk? I'd like to see that marvelous garden you have out front there."

"Of course." But truth journey or not, she was *not* going to divulge what had been buried underneath the garden prior to the renovations.

Esther breathed in the scents and said, "Just look at this! The water feature is quite impressive, Lorna. And the tiers, how ultimately creative! Was the garden here when you bought the property?"

"Uh, no. Milton designed it, and we all built it."

"Ah. Your caretakers are very efficient, I'm sure."

"Shall we sit down?"

Esther sat on one of the cement benches, and Lorna chose the one opposite so she could face her mother.

"So …" Esther lifted her chin. "… What made you embark on this little venture, Lorna?"

"The venture wasn't so little, but more on that later."

"Does your being a … lesbian have anything to do with this?"

"In a fashion, yes."

"Because when you decided to move down here, I thought it was most impulsive, and you're not an impulsive person. You've always been quite pragmatic and thorough."

"Yes, this is true. But, Mother, for most of my life, I've lived two lives."

"Again, what does that mean?"

"Who I was at home and at school was very different from who I was when I was alone."

"I don't understand. Was it because you knew from a young age you were … different?"

"Good Lord, Mother. It's not a disease. And yes, I knew from a young age something was different, but I didn't realize it until I met Jeanie."

"You two spent an inordinate amount of time together."

"She opened my heart. Colors and sounds and words came to life. I fell in love with her, Mother. Plain and simple."

Esther sighed. "But you seemed so well-adjusted!"

"Ah yes, the well-adjusted daughter. Always the well-adjusted daughter."

"You had anything and everything you could want! Clothes, vacations, cars, a top-notch education, a beautiful roof over your head, so many friends!"

"I did. I'm very grateful, Mother. Father was an amazing provider. But I had to have good grades to get into that top-notch school. I had to have the *drive* to show Father that I was just as capable and Norman and Gail. I had to be involved in school social and political events to uphold the Hughes name. I did all that. But it wasn't who I was inside."

"So why couldn't you be who you were on the inside at home?"

"Because neither one of you would have accepted it, and it had nothing to do with my proclivity."

"Then, what?"

"Do you know I used to spend almost every moment I could with a group of friends in Coventry?"

Esther guffawed, "The *Bohemians*?"

"Yep."

Esther grunted softly and looked around at the garden. "Well, I didn't see *that* coming, either."

Lorna leaned forward, "I usually kept a change of clothes in my car or stuffed into the back of my closet so I could ditch the penny loafers for soft shoes. And hats, skirts, flowing tops. I did it all, Mother. I even smoked pot."

Esther laughed, "Oh my."

Lorna looked at her. "If you saw me, you wouldn't have recognized me."

"So, why?"

"Because I related to artists, people who struggled. I saw how hard it was for them to make a living. They lived hand to mouth. Remember I asked you and Father to give some of your money to the Struggling Artists Coalition?"

She waved her hand, "Oh, I do. But to what end? Unless the artists went to school it seemed like a waste of money."

"Mother, the reason I joined the Greater Cleveland Arts Council was to appropriate funding for serious artists. And by serious, I mean people who *did* get an education, people who could barely make ends meet because of school loans. And not only artists, but writers and musicians!

"But the council fought me on my ideas saying it would be too expensive to fund housing," Lorna said. "And there weren't enough people to recruit to research potential candidates. So, I decided to take matters into my own hands and start this." She opened her arms to the rest of the property. "To give creative people a soft place to land and work at their chosen field."

Esther regarded her daughter. "Well, I'll be. A paradigm pioneer."

Lorna waited a moment to see if her mother was kidding. When she saw that she wasn't, Lorna said quietly, "Thank you." An odd sensation washed through her soul. Her mother had just paid her a genuine compliment. Something that rarely occurred while growing up. "Really. Thank you, Mother."

"You know, your father was very proud of your junior partner status and your graduating summa cum laude from his alma mater. You worked hard, Lorna; we both saw that. And I have to tell you I am sorry we did not see your ... other side."

Lorna had no words. She realized that her dominant persona—the one she maintained whilst growing up—was slowly fading. She hadn't had to utilize it on her own turf. She said, "You know mother. The Lorna you see right now is the Lorna I've always wanted to be since I could remember."

"And you couldn't see yourself finding love with a man?"

Lorna shook her head. "No."

They sat in silence for a while. "So, are your tenants also lesbian?"

"Yes."

"Well, it doesn't surprise me but how did you find

them?"

"I advertised."

"What, where? I mean—"

"In a newspaper called *Lesbian Connection*."

"I see."

Lorna looked around at her property. She loved the view from the tranquility of the garden. It kept her calm and focused.

"And are your tenants all artists?"

"Alice is an artist, Lindy is a graphic novelist, Mariella is a published writer, and PK is a musician."

"I assume these women will be at the Thanksgiving dinner?"

"Yes, they will."

"But what about their own families?"

"PK is not very close with her family, Alice doesn't want to return up north, Lindy's father is joining us, and Mari is just as happy to stay here for the holiday. We are starting to bond as a new kind of family."

"Okay. And whose father is it that's coming?"

"Lindy's. His name is Horace Sutton. From Atlanta. Quite well off, as I understand it."

"And what about her mother?"

"Died four years ago. Horace never remarried."

"Is he my age, would you say?"

"Mother."

"I'm just asking. I'd hate to be the only person here over fifty. Who else is coming?"

"Well, all of us, including Doreen. Steve Kent—he is a policeman for Heatherton County—and his girlfriend Jillian. Luis and Anita own a wonderful Mexican restaurant called El Mocambo in St. Augustine, and Cheenah Alvarez owns The Palms Motel up on route one just outside of St. Augustine. Anya, Luis, and Cheenah are related."

"Sounds like a rather large group. Where are you going to put everyone?"

"We rented tables and chairs. They'll be here tomorrow. We're going to move all the furniture around in the lobby and use the front desk as a buffet table. It'll be tight, but we're a cozy group."

"One would have to think."

Lorna waited for more questions. Instead, Esther heaved a loud sigh and stood up. "Well, I think we've covered several bases here. Perhaps a glass of wine is calling? How about we go get something to eat and drink and enjoy this beautiful weather?"

Lorna smiled for the first time since her mother's arrival. "I think that would be lovely, Mother."

Esther put her arm through Lorna's as they walked back to the main building. "It's going to take me a while to adjust to your life as it is now, Lorna. I hope you will understand that?"

"Of course."

"I thank you for being direct and honest. It certainly clears the air, wouldn't you say?"

"Yes, it does."

Esther leaned in as if to tell her a secret, "You know, maybe there are things about me that you don't know, either."

Lorna felt a bit giddy. "Really?"

"Yes, really."

"I'm intrigued, mother."

Esther laughed. "Let's go have that glass of wine."

Ellen Bennett

THIRTEEN

Dear Avril, November 29

Hi luv. I decided to write to you since we missed our phone call last week and will most probably miss it this week as well.

Wow. Where to start? Thanksgiving here at the motel was one for the books. Are you sitting down? My mother showed up three days before the holiday. Unannounced! I almost shit my knickers.

Then, as I am trying to recover from THAT, Doreen comes in through the kitchen door and calls for me with endearments like "honey" and "babe" because she had no idea Mother was here.

Well, as you can imagine, I had to tell Esther everything. She wasn't surprised. But you KNOW how I am when I'm not prepared! I guess, though, it was supposed to be that way. I did NOT, however, tell her about the bone findings. She was genuinely impressed with the garden. Let's leave it at that.

She invited herself to the Thanksgiving dinner I had planned for the tenants. I couldn't say no, could I?

So, Lindy invited her father, a widower named Horace. Horace Sutton! Handsome devil—reminds me of a young David Niven (including the little moustache). Well-dressed with ascots and shiny loafers. My mother wore a stylish kaftan, and Horace wore a sport jacket to dinner while the rest of us dressed for overindulgence. It reminded me of my parents when they dressed for a casual dinner of forty.

Esther zeroed in on him right away. He is right up her alley: rich (old family money), retired, AVAILABLE. They got along famously. I am glad he was there. He kept Esther entertained. I believe she enjoyed herself with someone closer to her age on hand. In fact, I believe she gave him her phone number! Oh God! Her phone number! I'll keep you posted.

The food—made mostly by Luis and Anya—was to DIE for. Esther insisted on buying the pies. She went a little hog wild (as Esther is known to do for "events"). Anya, Cheenah, Milton, Luis, Anita, Steve, and Jillian were there too! It was tight, but we managed. Once the beverages kicked in, it was magical. You would have had a grand time. Everyone was reasonably soused by the time the bonfire activities rolled around. But everyone behaved themselves.

On the Mariella/Cheenah front, I think there is a budding romance there. Cheenah had her hair cut and styled for Thanksgiving and even put on a little bit of makep. She looked pretty smashing I'd have to say! She's still nervous around Mariella, but Doreen agrees with me it will just be a matter of time. I would love to see Cheenah with a nice woman. She deserves it.

I'm sure you're wondering how Esther and Doreen got on. It was rocky at first. Esther thought Doreen was a bit masculine and asked me all kinds of questions regarding roles and whatnot. I explained that if I had wanted a man, I would have found one. I told her that Doreen was "all woman" and she shut her piehole after that. But when she saw Doreen's garage, she inserted herself as Doreen's new interior designer. She suggested red leather and chrome chairs with a small glass-top table in a "waiting area" with a coffeemaker for customers. Doreen, my girl and ever the "pleaser," kept giving me the stink-eye while appeasing mother. I thought it was kind of cute. I suppose it was Esther's way of reaching out. I might even go as far as to say that maybe mother was flirting with her a bit. DON'T SAY A WORD!

I think Esther liked the attention she got all the way around. The tenants enjoyed her stories—some I had never heard (like the time she and her friend made a papier-mâché replica of the principal of her high-school with overly large genitals, and drove it around on the back of Larry Epstein's convertible). I guess she was a bit of a rabble-rouser in her earlier days. Who woulda thunk?

Oh, you're going to love this. PK brought her guitar down to the bonfire after dinner, and guess who started singing with her? Cheenah! She has the voice of an angel! It was amazing. PK wants to write a few songs with Cheenah singing backup in the studio! Our Cheenah! Another case of who woulda thunk.

AND … here's the big news! Steve got down on one knee and proposed to Jillian! He was so nervous he dropped the ring at the edge of the bonfire. She said "yes"! And we all cried. Even Mother.

The wedding is next year in June. I know you and Saul will be on the guest list.

What else?

I have to say I am glad things turned out the way they did. Relief in the form of disclosure. I had to give Mother credit. She tried to understand how hard it was for me to live two lives while growing up. She never saw it but suspected "other agendas" as she put it when it came to Jeanie.

I know it will take time for her to understand that the motel represents more than just a venture. I'm still processing the reality of what I've accomplished here and why. Sometimes I think back to the first time I told you about the motel idea and how you said it was going to be "one big-assed mistake." There were times I thought you were right, even before the exhumation of the bodies. But I have to say, tenacity won out. And of course, you coming to my rescue during the excavation nightmare was key in me not losing my shit altogether! But those days are gone. The garden continues to be a light in my life. And I continue to connect my two lives together to be comfortable in my own skin.

Sometimes I miss Ellis. He was a good father in that he instilled solid values. He was smart, well-informed, and sharp when it came to business. I only wish we had been able to forge a stronger bond at the time of his death. But …

On a lighter note, I am heading to Miami with Doreen for Christmas to be with Vinnie and his boys. It sounds like it's going to be another one for the books. Vinnie is such a character—old Mafia skinny tough guy! Vinnie wants to meet me to make sure I'm good enough for his Doe!

I'll give you the full rundown when I see you. Doreen compared Betty Grable, (Vinnie's house manager, possible bed mate, ew) to Anya. I guess she's quite endowed, was very sexy in her time and takes no guff. Doreen said she was married once and has a grown son (who, by the way, is in love with Doreen—**double** ew). Sounds like Vinnie takes good care of her, tho.

Anyhoo, I will WOW them with my gleaming personality and charming good looks! How could they not approve? HAH, don't answer that!

I'll be heading to Cleveland right after New Year's. Doe and I will come back to the motel after Christmas to ring in the new year with everyone here, and Doe is going to run the show while I'm gone. Lindy is going to take Alice, PK, and Mariella with her for Christmas in Atlanta. They're all going to pile into the Mustang and head north. Would love to be a fly on the dashboard for THAT trip!

So, I want to see Saul and the kids, and maybe you and I can steal away for some much-needed girl time? Mother has plans for us. Dinner and theater at the Cleveland Playhouse, she's giving a speech for the new wing at the Cleveland Art Museum, dinner with Norman and Gail and their kiddos. It'll be the usual—busy busy.

Okay, I think this covers most of it. I hope your holiday went well with Saul's family. Please give him and the kids hugs all the way around. I miss you. Can't wait to see all of you!

Love you much,
L-

FOURTEEN
Saturday, January 3, 1981
The Pagoda Motel

While Lorna was in Cleveland, Doreen took the helm at the motel. There wasn't anything different for her to do but to watch over things as usual.

During a phone call with Lorna in Cleveland, Doreen said, "Hang on, someone's driving up." She stood up while holding the phone receiver. "Hmm. Looks like a Camaro. Kinda beat up." Then she murmured, "What a piece of shit."

"You concerned?"

She watched whoever was driving the car park it and get out from the driver's side. "Doesn't look familiar. Let me call you back after I find out what this is all about."

"You, my loyal watchdog. Love you."

"Love you too."

Doreen hung up the phone and walked outside to greet the woman.

"Hi there. What can I help you with?"

The woman said, "Oh hi there! I was just wondering if you had any available cabins."

"Well no, actually, we don't. They are all rented."

The woman nodded and looked around without making eye contact with Doreen. "Oh, that's too bad. My husband and I were hoping to stay here this winter for a month or two."

Doreen's hackles rose and she wasn't sure why. "Oh, I see. Have you stayed here before?"

"Well, no." She cleared her throat. "We heard about it from a friend."

Doreen nodded. "Uh huh. Well, sorry to say we're all booked up."

The woman appeared to Doreen to be nervous. She kept

looking behind her at the cabins. She asked, "Is it all right if I look around. It's so ... quaint. The garden is so beautiful."

Doreen watched the woman. "Well, I can show you around, but really there aren't any cabins available, so ..."

"Darn. He's going to be so disappointed. We really liked coming here. It's so private and quiet."

Doreen nodded, "The ownership has changed, and now the cabins are rented for the season."

The woman nodded again, "Well, I guess we'll have to find another place to stay."

Doreen, her arms crossed in front of her chest, said, "I'm sorry. There's another motel up on Route One called The Palms. They usually have rooms available there."

The woman hesitated. "Oh sure, I know where The Palms is."

Doreen nodded. "Well, have a good day. Sorry we couldn't be more helpful here."

The woman started to go back to her car. "Thanks anyhow."

Doreen watched as the woman started the engine, looked once more at the cabins, and slowly drove out of the turnaround.

Doreen saved the make and model of the Camaro in her head. Something about the whole transaction bothered her, and she wasn't sure why. Then it struck her. She stopped and muttered, "Wait a minute here. I thought she said she had never been here before, but then a minute later changed her tune that her husband would be so disappointed because they loved coming here."

She ran inside to call Cheenah at The Palms. When Cheenah answered, Doreen said, "Hey, I just turned someone away who was interested in renting one of the cabins for her and her husband. I told her we were booked and suggested she try your place."

"Is hokay. Will she come here now?"

"I don't know. But if she does, stall her and call me."

"What? Stall her? Like—"

"Just talk to her for a minute. You're good at that. It'll

give me time to fire up the bike and head over there. I want to follow her."

"Follow her?" When Doreen did not respond, Cheenah said, "Hokay. I will call you if someone comes in. What does she look like?"

"Short, big boobs. Teased bottle-blond hair, lots of makeup. Drives a tan Camaro."

"Tan Camaro, lots of boobs. Hokay. I will call you if I see this woman."

"Thanks, Cheen. You're the best."

"Ay."

Doreen had her doubts about the woman going to The Palms. She had the distinct feeling that there might be more to the story. Just what that was, she wasn't sure. But she would keep an eye out.

FIFTEEN
Sunday, January 4, 1981
The Pagoda Motel

Doreen turned in for the night. She had just done her routine "walk through" around the motel proper, enjoying the peaceful night air and gentle roll of the surf.

All was quiet. It was a cool night, in the fifties, so Doreen pulled an extra blanket out of the closet and grabbed Lorna's pillow, bringing it up to her nose. The scent calmed her.

Doreen woke up with a start and looked at the bedside clock. One thirty-four.

She leaned on her elbow, stock still, then sat up in bed, her sense of something amiss raising the short hairs on the back of her head.

She threw back the covers and listened again. Something like a clanking sound was coming from outside of the main building. A sound she had never heard before on the property. Her first thought was that a mechanical issue was at hand. But what? The main air conditioner was off. "The water pumps don't sound like that," she mumbled.

She jumped out of bed and put on a sweatshirt and sweatpants then slipped her feet into a pair of flip-flops as she made her way to the stairwell. She quickly went down the steps, stopping in the kitchen to retrieve a heavy-duty flashlight that Lorna kept in the utility closet.

She heard the sound again and stepped quietly out of the back door of the main building. She walked toward the source of the sound and ascertained that it was coming from her cabin, the first on the right of the circle.

"What the hell?" She whispered into the dark night.

As she neared her cabin, she saw Anya and Milton

walking toward her, a flashlight in Milton's hand but turned off.

She heard other sounds as well. Voices, in harsh rushed whispers, carrying through the night air.

"Miss Doreen," Anya hissed, "what is going on?"

Doreen approached them and whispered, "I have no idea. Woke up from a sound sleep. Traced the sound here."

"Us too," Milton explained, "we heard something very strange, and we did not know from where. I have never heard this sound before."

Doreen saw a glimmer of light come from the back of her cabin—as if someone had turned on a flashlight.

Her hackles rose. She felt a sudden chill.

"There's someone in my cabin."

Anya leaned forward, witnessing the same scene. "Yes, there must be to be making all this noise!"

Doreen thought about finding a baseball bat or some type of weapon.

They heard the sound again, then raised voices.

They moved forward in a pack.

Doreen whispered, "I'm going to go inside and try to surprise the intruders. You guys step around the back. If you hear anything that sounds like gunfire, call Steve."

"*Gunfire?*" Anya hissed. "But Miss Doreen—." Her eyes were wide.

Doreen shushed her. She whispered back, "Just do it."

Anya nodded reluctantly, then took Milton by the arm and stealthily moved toward the back of the cabin.

Doreen quietly moved up the front steps of her cabin, avoiding the known creaks in the wood, her heart pounding in her ears.

Whoever was in there was making a good deal of noise. She figured there was more than one person.

She swallowed hard and tried to calm her heart rate. She could use the flashlight as a weapon, but what if they had a gun?

The clanking continued in earnest. Doreen could not, for the life of her, figure out what was going on in there.

Then there came the sound of metal on metal, and the

distinct sound of a female voice saying, "Holy shit!"

Doreen took a deep breath, put her slightly shaking hand on the doorknob, then blasted through the door. She ran the few steps to the galley kitchen, slammed her hand on the light switch with a sweaty palm, and called out, "Freeze!"

When the bright overhead light illuminated the room, she could not believe her eyes. All she could manage to say, when she saw a woman who resembled the same woman who approached her yesterday inquiring about renting a cabin was, "*You*?!"

Then she heard a male voice from behind a black ski mask over his face say, "*You*?!"

Then silence.

Doreen blinked several times. "What the...?"

There was a hole in the floor of her kitchen about the size of a small dinette table. The refrigerator had been moved aside, and there was dirt and broken wood scattered around the hole. A large metal box with its lid snapped off was near the woman's feet.

Doreen looked back at them, her breath coming in rasps. When the man took off his face mask, Doreen felt herself sway. She caught herself on the back of a hastily strewn kitchen chair and muttered, "Please tell me this is a bad dream."

The man said, "Oh my God."

Doreen sputtered, "Georgie?"

The woman, who was still holding the flashlight on the contents of the metal box even though there was enough light to see, said, "This is the bitch I was tellin' you about!"

Georgie said with alarming calm, "Irene, meet my sister, Doreen. Doreen, meet Irene."

Doreen was speechless, her mouth agape. She looked again at the floor, at the metal box, at the dirt and tools used to pull the wood up from the floor beams, and then back at Georgie and Irene.

Anya and Milton ran into the cabin and stopped short of tumbling into Doreen. When they peered into the kitchen, Anya caught her breath. She murmured, "Oh, mi dios!"

Georgie said, "I can explain."

Doreen answered, "You've got three seconds before I call the cops."

Georgie pulled off his gloves and approached his sister. "No, no. Don't do that."

Anya stepped in front of Doreen. "I don't think so. Who are you and why are you here?"

Doreen pulled Anya back by the shoulder. She said, while never taking her eyes off Georgie, "This is my brother, Georgie, Anya."

Georgie attempted to approach again, and Doreen called out, "Just stay where you are, Georgie. Just stay where you are."

Irene said, "We can—"

Doreen shot her a glare, pointing her finger. "You don't get to talk right now. I knew there was something fishy about you when you just *happened* by yesterday. You stand there and keep your trap shut until I'm ready for you to talk."

Irene put her head down and raised her hand palm side out as if to make a truce. "Okay, Okay. Let's not get too crazy here."

Georgie put his hand on Irene's shoulder, "It's okay, babe. We're going to work this whole thing out. But first," he looked back at his sister, "what are *you* doing here?"

Doreen said, "I happen to live here."

"Then you knew about the money?"

"What money?"

Anya and Milton quietly gasped.

Georgie looked at them and said, "Who are they?"

Doreen said, "Don't you worry about who they are. They will call the police in two seconds if you try anything funny. They know about you."

"Great. Then we're all friends now."

"Hardly." Doreen surveyed the room. She put two and two together, quickly. The hole in the floor, the metal box with a tightly sealed package inside of it, slightly ripped open and revealing what was most likely money. "Are you fuckin' kidding me?"

"Look, I can explain."

Doreen reached for the phone. "Like I said."

Georgie put his hands out, "No, wait. Here's the deal. Irene got word that there was money hidden here from when Gino used the motel as a safe house."

Doreen cut in, "Who told *her* this?"

Irene jumped in, "One of my regulars at the diner where I—"

Doreen raised her voice, "I thought I told you to shut your trap!"

"Right, right. Sorry. I was just—"

Doreen shot her a glare before looking at Georgie again, "So, someone tells her there is money buried here. And who might that be, Georgie? Who is still alive to tell that story?"

"Uncle Vinnie."

Doreen gasped, "*Vinnie?*"

Milton whispered, "Oh no, Uncle Vinnie."

Georgie spoke quickly. "Yeah, see, Irene is the manager at the diner where Vinnie gets his breakfast. He likes to talk, Vinnie does, so he was telling her all kinds of stories about the family. Like how Gino and his boys would do business out of certain safe places, like this motel. Then he tells her about all this money that Gino hid in this cabin. I guess this was his cabin."

Doreen turned the chair around and sat down on it. Her mind reeled. "Go on."

"So he tells Irene that there is all this money buried here. That after Gino got knocked off, the family shut down the operations here and moved on to another location. And that Gino hid the money in a safe box under the fridge, in the floor."

Doreen ran her hand over her face and muttered, "Ah God."

"So, Irene got this idea and passed it on to me. We weren't sure about it, but according to Vinnie he was pretty sure the money was still here. And … and … look, Doe! It's here! Just like he said!" Georgie grabbed the box and brought it to Doreen.

Doreen turned away. All she could think about was how

to tell Lorna about this. She was shocked, flustered, and starting to feel anxious. She looked at the packages of sealed money.

Anya and Milton leaned in and peered over her shoulder, whistling at the contents of the box.

Doreen covered her eyes with her hand. She saw her present, her future, her life, flash by. It almost made her sick. She said, "Anya, Milton, I'm good in here. I need a few minutes alone with my brother. I'll holler if I need you."

Anya stood up, giving Georgie and Irene the stink eye. "I don't like these two. But I will go and wait for you."

Georgie shrugged his shoulders. "Hey, we're family. It's okay."

Anya said quietly, "You might be family but is not okay."

When Anya was out of earshot, Doreen sighed. "Georgie, sit down with me here." She indicated another chair, and he pulled it around to face her at the little table. "Good. Now." She looked at Irene. "Here's what needs to happen. First of all, Irene?"

"Yeah?"

"Do me a favor and reach into the second drawer there, the one to the right of the sink."

Irene furrowed her brows. "What for?"

Doreen did not look at her but kept her eyes on her brother. "Just do it, Irene."

Irene looked at Georgie. Georgie nodded, "Go ahead babe."

Irene said, "What am I lookin' for?"

"Duct tape."

She opened the drawer, rifled around a bit, and pulled out a roll of gray tape. "Now what."

Doreen explained, "Go ahead and measure out about four inches and tear off that piece."

Irene did as she was told. "Okay, now what?"

Doreen turned to look at her directly. "Put it over your mouth."

Irene cocked her head. "Are you outta your fuckin' mind?"

"No. Put the tape over your mouth and make some coffee. It's going to be a long night. You'll find everything where you think it should be. As a manager of a diner, you should know these things."

Irene shook her head. Georgie signaled for her to comply. She ripped off a piece of tape with a grunt, pulled it off her finger, and muttered, "This is insane. I can't believe I'm listening to this bitch."

Doreen ignored her and turned her focus back on her brother. She said, "Okay, Georgie. We got a real situation here, and I've got a few questions you need to answer."

Georgie said, "I don't owe you anything, Doe. Really, I don't."

Irene slammed the cupboard doors.

Doreen shot her a look. Irene narrowed her eyes and seemed to be breathing a bit heavy with the tape on her mouth. She gave Doreen the finger.

"Yeah, you do owe me. See, you're in my cabin here, a cabin I rent from the owner of this motel, and you've gone and dug up my floor and made a mess of things."

Georgie smugly responded. "I'll pay you to get it fixed up just like it was. It's kind of a dump anyhow. How did you end up here?"

"Here's the deal, Georgie. How are you going to pay for the repairs?"

He nodded towards the metal box. "Duh."

Doreen clucked. "I see."

Irene finally found the coffee and filled the glass pot with water from the sink.

Doreen took in a deep breath and sat back in her chair. "You're still the same old kid, aren't ya, bro? Twenty-seven and still a kid."

"I grew up while I was in the slammer, Doe. I'm not a kid any—"

Doreen leaned forward in a flash and grabbed him by the front lapels of his black jacket. He went to sit back but did not anticipate her strength. She yanked him close to her face.

Quietly, she said, "I have been watching you for years.

You're nothing but a two-bit punk. You've done nothing but disappoint the family, Georgie. I will give you that you are incredibly talented, but it stops there. You're inconsiderate. You take what you can get and run, and you think you can come in here and take what, frankly, is not yours."

Georgie looked at his sister with wide eyes. Irene stopped what she was doing, but when she tried to come to Georgie, Doreen put out her hand to stop her. She retreated to the counter.

"So, here's what's going to happen. When the coffee is ready ..." She peered here at Irene, who quickly turned the coffeemaker on, and continued, "... we are going to discuss, like adults, what your intentions are, were, with this money. Until that time, I will give you a pen and paper, and you will write down your parole officer's name and phone number." She released her hold on him, and he sat back, shrugging his shoulders back into his jacket.

"I don't have that information on me, Doe."

"Where is it?"

"Back at Irene's place in Miami."

"So, technically, you're already on the lam, right?"

"Well, no. I can't leave the state."

"You're already on the lam. I'm sure you thought you'd get this money and get the hell out of Dodge, is that right?"

The coffee started percolating. Irene leaned against the counter with her arms crossed tightly against the chest. She cleared her throat and pointed to the tape on her mouth.

"What?" Doreen asked.

Irene pointed to her groin. Doreen nodded. "Take off the tape but keep it quiet. The bathroom is around the corner there. If you try anything funny, I'll have the cops here so fast your ass won't have time to dry."

Irene nodded and yanked off the tape. She muttered, "This is just off the wall." Then she slammed the bathroom door behind her.

Doreen said, "Luckily the window is too small for her to get those fuckin' boobs through. Where didja find this one, anyhow?" Georgie had a reputation for having tough, slightly skeevy, women at his side.

"We been together about a year or so. I really love her, Doe."

"Yeah. So, what are your plans?"

"We're going to leave the country."

"Just like that, huh?"

"Yep."

"You gotta passport?"

"Not yet, but we gotta guy who'll get them for us."

Doreen shook her head slowly. "Jesus, Georgie. Don't you know you're asking for trouble?"

"How so? We leave, and no one can find us. We get new IDs, we're golden."

Doreen wanted to cry. She was tired, frustrated, a little nauseated, and ready for this nightmare to be over. She stood and paced. A part of her was fine with Georgie's plan. It was his life. She could get the kitchen repaired before Lorna's return. It would be over, and no one would be the wiser.

Except that Anya and Milton had witnessed the whole thing.

And Doreen knew Anya.

Doreen turned to face her brother. "Look. I know you and me haven't been very close over the years. You went one way with your life, and I went another. And that's okay. But this. There is so much more here that you don't know about."

Georgie nodded, "Just let us go and no one will be the wiser. Like you said, it's my life and whatever happens, happens, right?"

"No. Well, yes and no. There are two witnesses. And they are very close with the owner of the motel."

"Well, where *is* the owner?"

"She's out of town. I'm in charge when she's out of town."

"So, tell your Mexican pals to keep it quiet."

"It doesn't work that way."

Irene emerged from the bathroom. She entered the room and said, "Let's just get the money and get the hell out of here, Georgie. Your sister can't keep us here."

"Come on, Doe."

Doreen studied her brother. For a moment she felt her resolve dissolve. He was a stranger, yet there were so many familiarities to their lives. A part of her wanted to reach out and pull him in, rehabilitate him. Another part wanted him to act on his desire to leave the country, never to be heard from again. Her life was going along so well—the garage, her relationship, her new friends. She was putting down roots. And she didn't want those roots jeopardized by her non-law-abiding brother.

But then again, there was a large stash of money. Lots of it, tax free. And Anya and Milton had witnessed the whole thing. It wasn't merely between her and her brother.

Doreen sat down again. "We gotta figure this out. There is no way I can keep this from the owner. There is more history here than you know about, Georgie. More than you can imagine."

Georgie seemed to soften. "Look Doe, whatever that is, it doesn't involve us. Maybe you could tell your Mexican friends that we split up the money, took our share, and left."

"Look, I need to think."

"So...think! We'll help you clean up and take off! No harm, no foul."

Doreen looked up at him. She was amazed. "You really think it's all right to come in here, make a fuckin' mess, take something that might not be yours, and then leave? With *me* holding the bag? Is *that* how you think this should go down?"

"Well."

Doreen stood up again, "Well, nothin'! When you decided to start your little crime spree adventures, Vinnie did everything he could to keep you out of jail. But you went along as if no one or nothing else mattered. You didn't care who you hurt."

"What are you talkin' about, Doe?"

"Your life! Our life!"

"Our life was doomed from the get-go. Let's not forget that!"

"Yeah, it was. But why couldn't you stay out of trouble?"

Georgie stopped and looked at his sister. "You know,

maybe you had it a little easier than me. Maybe everyone liked you better because you're smarter than me. Maybe—"

Doreen cut him off, "Do you have any idea how talented you are?"

"Yeah, sure! And where the *fuck* did *that* get me? Huh, Doe?"

"You could have—"

Georgie cut her off. "Have what? What did that get me?"

Doreen nodded and sighed. "I know."

Doreen thought about all the times her father called him a sissy, a pussy. Not a real man. Just because he was good at art.

She said, "You know, you could use the money to go back to school."

Irene laughed, "Oh brother. And will that do?"

Doreen shot her a withering glare. "Shut it."

Georgie said, "Sure. Go back to school. For what?"

"Learn how to do your art the right way, the honest way."

Georgie chuckled, "With dirty money. Yeah. That makes sense."

"Well it's no different than runnin' all over the world like a big shot. The money's gonna run out. Then what?"

Irene said, "We are planning on getting jobs."

Doreen turned to face her, "Oh, I see. That's brilliant. Your boyfriend has a record. How the hell is he going to get out of the country? How the hell is he going to get a legal passport? And what makes you think the state of Florida isn't going to hunt him down? He's evading parole."

"There are people who can get us what we need."

Doreen shook her head and looked at her brother. "Don't do this, Georgie. Don't do this. You've got to stop somewhere."

For a moment, there wasn't a sound in the room aside from them breathing.

"Why, look who finally cares!" Georgie mumbled.

Doreen leaned forward, "I do care. You're family. Granted you've put some good wedges all around, but we're family."

"So, let me get this right. You think you did things right, right? So, you finished high school and then when you turned eighteen you got your money and you were outta there. On your big-assed bike. Just roamin' the countryside. Did you work? Did you get a job?"

"I worked a little. But that's not the point. I never did anything that got my ass thrown in prison."

Georgie snorted. "So what?"

"Yeah, what makes you so high and mighty?" Irene asked. "I work hard for my money."

"All I'm sayin' here, Georgie, is that maybe you have a chance here. An opportunity to make things right."

"Sure, right in your world, but not in mine. What am I going to learn at school, huh? I've already got the talent."

"But it's raw talent. If you go through the right channels, you could take it to the moon!"

"What are you talkin' about, right channels?"

Doreen took in a deep breath and let it out. "Look, if you go back to school, the state would be on your side. They'd see you as rehabilitated. You don't have to keep on running, Georgie. It's going to catch up with you and you know it. It'd be a matter of time until you get caught. Then what?"

"And you're such a big authority on all this? When did *you* ever stop runnin'?"

The question stopped Doreen in her tracks. How was she going to explain all this to her brother? How was that going to work?

She took a deep breath then let it out. "Look. Do whatever you want, Georgie. I can't stop you."

Irene piped in. "She's right. Let's take the money and get back on the road. We can make Miami by mid-morning."

Georgie stood up, "Yep. You're right, Reenie. Let's get the money and go."

Doreen sat still. She had no fight left in her.

She watched as Georgie tried, but failed, to shove the dirt and wood into some sort of organized pile with his foot.

Irene picked up the metal box containing the money and said, "Let's get a move on it, Georgie. C'mon."

Georgie looked at his sister, a flicker of something in his eyes.

Doreen asked, "What?"

He sighed, shook his head then said, "Nothin'."

Doreen wasn't sure if it was the glory of her surrender or something deeper and less accessible.

She watched them leave the cabin without another word.

The refrigerator clicked on. Doreen snorted. "At least they had the brains to keep it plugged in."

She sighed deeply and assessed the mess in her kitchen.

Her throat was thick, her heart heavy.

She walked to the wall phone, picked up the receiver, punched in 9-1, and stopped, returning the receiver to its cradle, thereby ending the attempted call.

"Ah God." Sobs wracked her chest. Tears ran freely. She grabbed a kitchen towel and howled into it.

As Doreen buried her face in the towel Anya entered the cabin and went directly to her. "Oh, mi dios! Miss Doreen, come!" She held her arms open. Doreen fell into them.

Anya cooed. "Now, now. That's right. Let it all out now. That's right."

Doreen sobbed until she had nothing else to give. She backed up, blew her nose into the dish towel, and sat down heavily in a chair.

Anya took the dish towel and tossed it into the sink. She grabbed a mug, poured coffee into it, and pulled another chair around to face Doreen. "Let's talk about this, no?"

Doreen nodded and whispered, "Yeah. You know, it wasn't enough that my grandfather, mister big Mafia kingpin, killed those men," she scowled, "and buried the bodies on the property. But now this?"

Anya cooed, "I know I know. But this is all in the past, and thankfully, Miss Lorna. Let us explain how we all knew about it and wanted to get it out in the open, once and for all."

Doreen hung her head. "I'm just …"

Anya changed the subject. "I saw your brother and his lady friend leave. Did they take the money?"

"Yeah."

"Did you call the policia?"

"No."

"Don't you think you should?"

Doreen cleared her throat. "No. It's his life. It's not like he robbed a bank. If the officials want him bad enough, they'll find him." She added with a sigh. "I don't want anything to with it, or him."

Anya nodded. "You want some coffee?"

"Something stronger."

She stood, walked into her little living room and opened a small cabinet.

"I need this right now." Doreen unscrewed the cap on the bourbon bottle and took a swig.

Anya whistled, "Ah, good. Take another sip now."

Doreen sat down heavily. "I can't believe this." She took another pull. "I mean, my fuckin' family just keeps oozing up outta the woodwork."

Anya nodded, "Yes, miss. Again a few feet in the dirt."

Doreen chuckled. "Yeah, we like to bury things."

"This is true," Anya agreed.

"What the hell. I mean, look at this mess!"

Anya said, "We can fix like new, if not better."

"Lorna comes back in two days. What the hell am I going to tell her?" Doreen looked at Anya. "She's going to tell me to pack my bags."

"You think?"

"Why wouldn't she? Huh? She's already dealt with crime on her property because of *my* screwed-up family and now ..."

Anya cocked her head, sipped her coffee. "Well, not really a crime. No one has been killed. Just a box of money."

"My delinquent brother and his half-brained girlfriend with the big tits."

Anya shrugged and nodded. "Well, yes. She has a good endowment."

Doreen sighed heavily. "Aw God, Lorna's gonna ..." She took another sip. "She's going to tell me to hit the road, and I wouldn't blame her."

Anya leaned forward, "No, I don't think she will do that.

I think she loves you very much, and I think she will talk first."

Doreen continued. "I'm like a stain that you can't get out."

"No, Miss Doreen. You are not a stain. You are a *very good* woman, you are. I'll admit, at first, we all had our fears, but now you give so much love to Miss Lorna. You are not a stain. Maybe your family gave you the stain, but you are not a stain."

"Thank you, Anya. I know coming from you it's real."

"We love you, Miss Doreen."

Doreen stood up and paced. "I don't have to tell her. I could just let this go and ..."

Anya shook her head. "And, what? Yes. You must tell her. It will eat away at you if you don't. I know this from much experience."

Doreen looked at Anya and nodded. "You're right. It would eat away at me every second of every day. I have to tell her. I have to step up and tell her and accept whatever she says to me. And I'm scared shitless."

"Why are you scared, Miss Doreen?"

Doreen leant against the kitchen counter and crossed her arms at the chest. "Because I don't want to disappoint her. I don't want her to have to make the decision to kick me to the curb."

Anya reached for the bourbon bottle. "Mind?"

"Help yourself."

"Miss Lorna will not kick you in the curb. I think her love for you is very strong. I can see that. She might get mad, but she won't kick you away." Anya poured a snort of bourbon into her coffee.

"I can't believe this happened. My family. The gift that keeps on giving. I wonder what else is underfoot?" Doreen tapped her foot on the floor.

"Let's hope this the end of it, si?"

"God, let's. Well, I think I need to go to bed and sleep. Maybe I'll wake up later and this will all have been a bad dream."

Anya drained her coffee, stood up, and rinsed the mug out in the sink. "I think this will be a wise movement, Miss Doreen. I left Milton snoring on the couch. I think I am better watchdog than him. Later today we will look at the floor and decide how to fix it."

"Thank you, Anya."

Anya squeezed Doreen's shoulder. "It will all be hokay."

Doreen reached out and hugged her. "You are one special lady, my friend. I know you've got my back."

"We will always have our backs together, comprende? Remember, you fixed up my van and now it runs like new."

Doreen flicked the switch, and the cabin went dark. She shut the door behind them and wished Anya goodnight.

The night air was brisk; she felt a chill. She stopped and closed her eyes. Things had been going along so well. Her garage was almost done. Alice was putting the finishing touches on the mural. Her heart was in the right place, she loved where she lived, and she was in love with a woman who gave her the room to grow.

But something kept surfacing from her solar plexus, and tonight it was almost impossible to swallow it back down.

Doreen whispered vehemently. "Go. Get out of my head. I don't need you anymore." Then, after a long breath in and exhalation out, weaker and pleading: "Please, just … leave me the hell alone."

SIXTEEN
That same night
3 a.m.

Lindy stealthily walked up the steps to Alice's cabin. She wrapped her knuckles lightly on the wooden screen door. She could hear Alice snoring softly from within the cabin.

She tried the door and found it unlocked. She called out in a harsh whisper, "Alice?"

Nothing,

"Alice?" She tiptoed into Alice's bedroom area. A nightlight bathed the room in a soft glow.

Alice was on her side, a Coke can and journal on her small nightstand. Lindy leaned over, making sure not to jostle the can. "Alice, wake up."

Alice stirred, then sat up quickly when she realized someone was standing next to the bed.

"Whaaa?"

Lindy sat down on the edge of the bed, "It's just me, hon. Lindy."

Alice instinctively reached out for her, "Oh, hi babe. Wanna get in?"

Lindy said, "No." She rolled her eyes. "I need you to sit up."

Alice rustled and brushed her hand over her face. "Is everything okay? You okay?"

Lindy nodded, "Yes, I'm fine. But I gotta tell you what I just witnessed. You're not going to believe this."

Alice shook her head. "Am I dreaming? You want to tell me that something happened that I won't believe? What? What time is it?"

"Almost three-fifteen."

"It's a.m., right?"

"Yeah."

"Oh brother. Well, I need some water. I have a glass in the fridge. Would you get it for me? I gotta pee."

When Alice came back to bed, Lindy was sitting on the end, the water glass crammed in on the nightstand.

"Thanks." Alice downed almost the whole glass. "So, what's so earth-shattering?"

"Well first, you're going to have to understand that what happened is only the tip of the iceberg."

"Okay."

"Doreen, our very own Doreen, is Mafia."

Alice snorted, "What the hell are you—"

"No, listen!"

The story came out without punctuation, a hurried run-on sentence that left Alice speechless.

"Let me get this straight. A strange sound woke you up after one o'clock in the morning. You went to the window in your kitchen because the sound seemed to be coming from that direction."

"Right."

"Then you heard voices coming from Doreen's cabin. Then this crazy incident happens. Are you sure you didn't just dream this?"

"No way, no how. Every word of it is true, I wrote it down in my journal. Her family was big into the Mafia, and her brother unearthed a box of money—apparently buried there many years ago by someone who must have been a kingpin or something. I think it was her grandfather!"

Alice belched quietly. "Humph." She scratched her head and looked at Lindy. "So, what now?"

"I think we need to learn more about this place is what I think."

"Like … what?"

"I'd like to learn the history of this motel. Something tells me there is a much bigger story here than just a woman who wanted to open a refuge for starving artists."

"Well, okay. How are you going to do that without ruffling a bunch of feathers? Doreen is tight-lipped. She keeps to herself a lot. Doesn't talk much about her past, except that her father died when she was young ... of a heart attack."

Lindy nodded her head. "Uh huh. Maybe not a heart attack...exactly."

Alice waved her off. "Look, this is pretty interesting but what are we going to learn now at three o'clock in the morning?"

"I think we should investigate this. It could be great fodder for the book I'm working on."

Alice raised her eyebrows. "You might want to think about that for minute. From what you said, Doreen sounded pretty upset."

"She was. But you can't make this shit up."

***

Later that morning at the motel

A ringing phone woke Doreen out of a very sound sleep. She jumped out of bed and wondered where the phone was. She almost dropped the receiver.

"Hello?"

"Hi, babe."

"Oh. Hi ... babe."

"Are you all right? Did you just wake up?"

Doreen fought down what she hoped was just a bad dream. "Yeah, didn't sleep so hot last night. Probably getting my period."

"Ah. Yep, I got mine yesterday so you should be getting yours any minute now."

Her nerves were on edge already. She tried to sound nonchalant. "How's everything in Cleveland?"

"Mom is going to sell the house and move down to Boca. I can't believe it. Our house ..."

"Well, you said it's too big for just her."

"It is. But it's the place where I grew up. It doesn't seem possible to pack this place in boxes and move."

Doreen could not sit still. She took the phone with her

while she paced. She looked out the window toward the ocean. It was a gray day, and the storm clouds looked ominous from the east. The Atlantic waters heavily moved whitecaps toward the beach, and a damp staleness permeated the air.

Just the way she felt.

Heavy and adrift.

Lorna was talking about something. "Honey, you really don't seem like yourself. Is everything okay? The motel?"

"Huh? It's pretty quiet around here." Doreen felt her throat close.

"Why don't you call me later when you're feeling better?"

"I think I'll do that. I'm just out of sorts. Yeah, you know how it gets sometimes around our cycles and stuff."

Lorna purred. "Well I can tell you one thing. I've missed you bad. I can't wait to see you and wrap myself around you."

Doreen felt her heart skip a beat. She tried to sound lighter than she felt. "I know. I miss you like crazy. It's going to be good to have you back home again. Well, home here, anyhow."

"It *is* my home, honey."

Doreen had to go to the bathroom. "How about I call you a bit later?"

"Okay, babe. Take a nice long walk on the beach. That always seems to help."

Doreen went to the bathroom, splashed some cold water on her face, and went downstairs to make some much-needed coffee.

Doreen carried her mug out of the main building and found Anya tending to her own little garden.

"Ay! Miss Doreen. I went to your cabin this morning with Milton, and we can fix the problem easily. The boards, we can get new boards and take away the broken ends. They will be a different color, of course, but they will be under the refrigerator."

"Thanks, Anya. I'm headed there now to start cleaning up the mess."

"We cleaned up a bit already. If you need anything, just holler, okay?"

"Thanks."

Doreen entered her cabin. "Shit …" She sighed quietly. She started moving the fridge aside, and the table and chairs to the edge of the room. She peered inside the hole in her floor. "Damn it all."

She picked up the phone and dialed Vinnie.

SEVENTEEN
Monday, January 5, 1981

Vinnie blew a gasket. He yelled, "What the hell is he thinking?"

Doreen held the phone away from her ear. "I don't know. He's really gone off the deep end here."

"If I get my hands on that little shit …"

"Listen, Vin, I don't care what you do with him, but make sure he doesn't come back here. Ever."

"Okay, Doe. But what about the money?"

"Don't care," she said emphatically.

"Well …" Lingering silence, then. "You all right?"

"I can't do it, Vin. I don't want any part of the family history, or the money, or …" She moved the mouthpiece away from her lips. She thought she might choke. Her mouth felt like a sock full of sand.

Vinnie talked a mile a minute about what he was going to do to Georgie. Doreen couldn't listen to it anymore. She told Vinnie she'd call him later.

When Doreen hung up the phone, panic engulfed her. She struggled to fight down the darkness that had historically propelled her to run. The urge was strong.

The inside of her chest felt like quills from a porcupine. Pinpricks reached out to her limbs and slid underneath her diaphragm. They sparkled behind her eyes and lingered in her gut.

She ran out of her cabin, knocked on Anya's door, and informed her she was going to take off on the bike. She threw her wallet into a backpack, grabbed her helmet and goggles, and fired up the Harley.

She blew north on A1A despite the dark clouds. The sound of the engine beneath her, the control of speed in her right palm, and the euphoria of conquering the open road eventually eased the sharpness of the quills.

She felt every single nuance: the grit of the road on her exposed skin, the stale air as it caught underneath her helmet, and the damp fog at the edge of her goggles.

Her busy mind finally settled as she leaned into the gentle curves along the seacoast road, feeling her body mechanics become one with the machine.

Farther up the road, the damp salt air became heavier and permeated her skin, nostrils, and eyes. Whitecaps broke closer to shore, and the asphalt smelled strongly sulfurous. She knew this meant rain, and lots of it.

She remembered that there was an abandoned diner/drive-in up the road a bit, so she gunned the engine. A flash of light followed by a loud crack of thunder came from behind her. She could see the busted sign of the diner about a hundred feet away.

"Shit." Water droplets plopped around her. She pulled into the parking lot and saw another biker standing next to his ride underneath the tin awning of the drive-in. She pulled in next to him to take cover.

A wall of water descended upon them as she slipped off her helmet and goggles.

He was smoking a cigarette, watching her. "You got here just in time."

Doreen swung her leg over the bike, then squeegeed the water off her arms. "You got that right."

The man looked out at the ocean. "Well, it's Florida. Usually hits like a motherfucker and then the sun comes out and bakes the road dry in short order." He took another long pull from his cigarette. "Where ya headed?"

"Just out for a ride. You?"

He made a quiet guttural sound and tipped his head toward his motorcycle. "Anywhere she takes me."

Doreen checked out his bike. Harley Road King. Big fairing, deep saddle, powerful engine. He had two large saddlebags strapped over the passenger seat and a smaller tour pack trunk that looked like an add-on. A stuffed backpack was at his feet.

He reminded her of herself.

Another flash of light and jolt of thunder surrounded them.

She stole another glance at him. "So, you just travelin' around then?"

He nodded and flicked his cigarette out into the rain. It sizzled and plopped to the ground. "Yep. Just ... travelin'."

He turned to look at her. "You live around here?"

"Down the road about ten miles. You?"

He cocked his head towards the bike, "Like I said. I live wherever she takes me." He picked up his backpack and fished around inside before pulling out a pack of cigarettes. "You want one?"

"No thanks, don't smoke."

He lit up. "Yeah. The old lady said I smoked too much, wanted me to give it up but...well, she gave up on me first."

"Oh man. Sorry to hear."

"Yeah. She died three months ago." He turned away from her.

Doreen looked at the man. He was older than she had initially thought. Maybe in his sixties. His beard covered leather-tanned skin, and a paunch sporting a Harley T-shirt hung over his belted jeans. His boots were worn at the left toe—the shifting foot—and his hands shook a little. His grayish black hair was short underneath a plain baseball cap, his neck tanned from riding away from the sun.

When the man turned to face her, she saw that his eyes were red. Her initial impulse was to go to him, put a hand on his shoulder, something.

She stood still.

He said, "Well, here I am, cryin' like a little boy."

"Nothing to be sorry for. Wanna talk about it?"

He shrugged. "What's to talk about? She had the cancer. Found it too late. She went kinda fast."

Doreen shook her head. "I am so sorry."

"Yeah." He sucked hard on his cigarette. "We was gonna ride out to the West Coast together. She had a bike, too. It was our plan to get on the road and see where it took us. But now ..."

Doreen understood completely. She felt for this man because now that his woman was gone, the road was his only ally.

The rain continued to pelt the tin roof. She didn't know what to say because anything she could have said would have been to admit to her own life, her own relationship with the road. Her own need to put miles between her and whatever she left behind.

Only he came by his honestly.

She knew, from that moment, she did not.

She blurted out, "I'm a runner."

He turned to look at her. "A what?"

She shook her head. "Never mind."

He nodded and went back to staring out over the shoreline. He sighed. "Well, the sky looks like it's gonna clear a bit. I think I might get back on the road. Can't stand still for too long these days."

Doreen knew exactly what he meant. "What's your name?"

"Al. What's yours?"

"Doreen."

He smiled slightly, "Well, Doreen. I hope you have a good ride wherever you're headed." He crushed out the spent butt with his foot and settled the backpack over his shoulders. He swung his leg over the chassis of the big bike and righted it center, kicking up the stand as he did so. Before he turned the key, he looked directly at her and said, "You got loved ones where you live, Doreen?"

She nodded. She could barely talk. "Uh hmm."

He leaned a bit towards her, "Then you make sure you love them every day all day. And you make sure you let them love you too because after they're gone, all you got left is your pain."

Doreen couldn't speak.

Al turned the key, and the engine roared to life. He gave it a bit of gas before shifting into first gear. He said, over the din, "Safe runnin', girl." Then he sped off out from under the tin roof, away from the temporary shelter, away from her.

She watched him turn left out of the parking lot and listened as he revved the engine through the first three gears to get up to speed. She whispered, "Safe runnin', Al."

The sun did come out, and as predicted the ground beneath her feet steamed and started to bake. Doreen walked out and crossed the road to the shoreline. There was no one or anything around for miles. She felt more alone than she ever had—even when traversing the country on her bike.

When she got to the beach, she sank down onto her knees and felt the vomit rise. With every muscle clenched, she brought up the contents of her stomach—which was not much since she had not eaten in almost twelve hours. She retched until there was nothing left but spit.

Afterward she collapsed onto her back. She felt as if her insides were pulling loose from their foundation. She couldn't stop shaking.

Between deep gulps of breath, pictures flashed like filmstrips behind her closed eyes. Her father, mother, brother, life, exes, people she had wronged and hurt, lies she had created to keep herself functioning on the run. Away from anything that resembled commitment. Away from anyone who tried to love her.

She sat up, lightheaded but better.

"Go home." Al's voice resonated in her head. "Go home and love your family."

EIGHTEEN
Same day
St. Augustine

Lindy charmed the elderly lady at the front desk of the St. Augustine Public Library.

"Oh, I just love your scarf. It's so colorful."

The attendant smiled and fingered the scarf, "Oh! Well, thank you. My granddaughter gave it to me for Christmas. It's so light on such a dreary day!"

"Indeed, it is!"

"What can I help you with, ma'am?"

Lindy leaned in. "Well, you see, I'm on a bit of a mission. I'm a writer and I'm looking to do a short story on your lovely town. It's for a travel magazine, you see."

The attendant nodded. "Oh sure. We get a few people in here looking for things to write about. But I'd say the best way to write about our beautiful town is to go outside and see it all for yourself!"

"Well, I can certainly appreciate that. And I have been around town. It's charming! But I think I'd like to look through old newspapers to see if there is anything exciting to write about. Like, history, or ..."

"Oh, I see. Well let me take you back to the microfiche machine. You can scroll through the newspapers that way. Have you ever used a microfiche machine before?"

Lindy thought, *what, does she think I was born yesterday?* "I think so!"

"What year are you interested in?" The attendant scuttled in front of Lindy. "I can set you up with a few if you need."

"Well, how about this past year? I can start there and go back if nothing sounds interesting to write about."

The attendant frowned. "What kind of interesting things

are you looking for? This is a small town, and not much happens. Maybe the yearly festivals and so on."

"Well, what about that old motel up on route A1A. Anything interesting ever happen over there?"

The attendant cocked her head. "A motel ... well, there was a little bit of scuttlebutt back last year about an excavation project gone wrong, but the police were very tight-lipped about it. Wouldn't let any reporters up there. Some gal from up north wanted to renovate it. To be honest, I think most people have forgotten about it. The motel is way out there over the ancient bridge. She may even have sold it."

Lindy felt her excitement gather. "Oh, I wouldn't know about that, but it might interesting. You know, a point of history for someone to visit."

The librarian waved her hand, "Oh, there's nothing to see over there but some broken-down buildings. Nothing a tourist would spend their time on."

Lindy was getting tired of the old biddy. "Well, how 'bout I go ahead and look through the old newspapers to see if something grabs my attention?"

"Suit yourself." She showed Lindy how to load the cassette and move the levers.

When Lindy finally had the space to herself, she began her search.

She didn't find anything particularly exciting; the attendant was right. The town was a complete bore—until she happened upon a small article dated June 26, 1980:

LET'S MAKE NO BONES ABOUT IT!

The sleepy little hamlet of Heatherton County isn't so sleepy this morning! An unusual discovery was made two days ago at the newly renovated Pagoda Motel. Owner Miss Lorna Hughes, Esq., of Cleveland, Ohio, was shocked to find out that buried underneath her recently excavated badminton court were human remains.

Earl Driver, of Earl Driver and Sons Excavation, was the first to see the find. He states that he and his crew were at the property to dig out an area for a new garden.

"When we got there, the asphalt had been removed and we just started hammering down. The first chunk came out at about four feet. As soon as we were able to get the big equipment in there to yank

it all up, we found the bones."
Miss Hughes was not available for comment. Local policeman, Officer Steve Kent, said, "What has happened here is a shock to us all." Local FBI were reluctant to comment as well but did say that the remains were under investigation.
Also found underneath the swimming pool was an old rusted van. It is purported that the van with New Jersey plates was used to bring the bodies to their final resting place at The Pagoda Motel.
Further reports will be forthcoming.
Pictured below:
The pit where the bodies were uncovered.

Roger Franklin, Reporter at Large

She nodded her head and said to herself, "I knew it!" She continued her search all the way through until December 31, 1980, but found nothing more.

On her way out of the library she thanked her lucky stars that the attendant was busy with other library members checking out books. She scooted past the line and made her way down the steps and onto the sidewalk.

Alice had been waiting for Lindy on a park bench in the middle of town.

"So? You find anything?"

Lindy sat down next to her. "Yep. Bones."

"Bones?"

"Buried at the motel."

Lindy recounted the article while Alice's eyes grew big. "Holy shit. So … wow. Do you think this has anything to do with Doreen?"

"I don't know, but I'm guessing so."

When Doreen arrived back at the motel, it was close to dinner time. She went to her cabin only to find Anya and Milton hammering boards onto the floor beams. The dirt was gone.

"Wow," she exclaimed.

Anya stood up, "I think we matched the floor wood, no?"

"It's pretty amazing."

"I know it looks to be newer than the other wood. The other is scuffed up, but I think it won't matter very much since the fridge is going to be over it, donchu think?"

"I do."

Anya studied Doreen. "You look to be very tired, Miss Doreen. Have you had any food today yet?"

Doreen shook her head. "No, but I'm pretty hungry now. You two eat yet?"

"Come, we will let Milton finish, and I will feed you. I made stew this afternoon."

Doreen took Anya by the shoulders and hugged her. Anya hugged her back. "All will be okay, Miss Doreen. You will see."

Doreen held Anya and spoke. "I just felt like giving you a hug. You are so special to me. You're like family. You know?"

"Yes. I do. And we are."

NINETEEN
Same Day

Alice and Lindy decided to have dinner at Mac's Crab Shack after the library jaunt.

"I wonder how Lorna met Doreen. She's not really the artist type."

"I think Lorna mentioned that Doreen happened upon the motel one day by mistake, or something to that effect."

Lindy pursed her lips. "A mistake? The place is totally off the beaten track. I mean …"

"Well, maybe it's not for us to know that right now."

"Well, I for one want to know all about it." She stood up. "I have to repair to the ladies' room."

The ladies' room at Mac's was barely short of an outhouse. Alice would have liked to have been a fly on the wall when Lindy went to repair.

Lindy returned to the table and sat down heavily. "Gawd, what a shithole. I thought I was going to lose my lunch at one point. Man. Squat, let it rip, wipe, then get the hell out."

Alice grimaced. "Pretty much."

Lindy opened a fresh Wet-Nap and aggressively wiped her hands. "But the food is top notch. I've never eaten such fresh fish."

Alice finished her beer. "Listen. I was thinking. Maybe you ought to put this bone-finding thing aside for now. From what you said, Doreen was upset last night. Maybe now isn't the best time to lampoon all that stuff. After all, Lorna never told us about it. I figure if she wanted it to be public knowledge with us, she would have said something."

Lindy waved her hand, "I'm not going to do anything sinister, Alice. I think the history of the motel is rather interesting, and it makes for good entertainment."

Alice knew she was fighting a losing battle. Lindy was headstrong, determined to get to the real story.

Alice shrugged. "Do whatcha gotta do."

***

Later that evening at the motel

The phone in the lobby rang. Doreen was getting out of the shower. She was exhausted.

"Pagoda Motel, this is Doreen."

A loud voice on the other end of the phone screeched. "Doreen, it's me, Betty. Vinnie's had a heart attack."

Doreen pulled the towel up close to her body. *"What? When?"*

Betty spoke quickly. "He was out on the veranda. He said he didn't feel well at dinner. Thought it was gas. When I went to check up on him, he had fallen out of the lounger and was half conscious. I called nine-one-one, and by the time they got here he was having the attack."

Doreen stood stock still. "Is he dead?"

"Not yet. But the doctors aren't sure he will make it through the night. Will you come?"

Doreen couldn't answer. Lorna was due back in the morning, and Doreen planned to pick her up at the airport in Jacksonville. "I ..."

Betty said, "Doreen!"

Doreen snapped to. "Of course, I'll be there. It's going to take me at least six hours to get down there, if not more. But if I leave now ..." Her exhaustion now replaced with terror. She could not imagine losing Vinnie. Not on top of everything that had gone on. She was too raw.

After they spoke for another moment, Doreen let the handset dangle in her hand. "This can't be happening." She hung up the phone.

Anya decided that Doreen must take her van. "You will not ride the motorcycle down to Miami right now. It is too late and too dark. It is not safe. You are upset of course. I know Miss Lorna would want it that way."

Doreen was finding it hard to put her thoughts together. She finally said, "Thanks, Anya. Will you please call Lorna in the morning and tell her? It's too late to call now."

"Yes, and if Miss Lindy cannot pick Miss Lorna up, I will take Miss Lorna's van to go to Jacksonville."

Doreen hugged her. "I don't know how to thank you during all this." She stepped back from Anya. "You won't say anything, will you, about what happened? I can't tell her yet. Not until I know more about Vinnie."

Anya nodded and pushed Doreen out the door. "Of course I won't. It is your story anyhow. Now, here is the rest of the beef stew you can eat cold if you get hungry. And you have a jug of water?"

"I do."

"Let us know when you get there. We will pray."

"Thanks, Anya."

TWENTY
Tuesday, January 6, 1981

At eight-thirty in the morning, Anya phoned Lorna. "Hello, Miss Lorna, it is Anya."

"Anya? Is everything okay?"

"Well, everything here at the motel is fine. But Miss Doreen had to go quickly down to Miami to see Uncle Vinnie. He had a heart attack last night."

"Oh my God, why didn't someone call me?"

"It was quite late, and Miss Doreen didn't want you to be concerned. I made her take my van and not the motorcycle. She was so upset. She told me to call you now, which I am doing of course, and tell you that Miss Lindy will pick you up at the airport at one o'clock today."

"Well I'm glad you insisted on the van. But ..."

"I know. It was so quick, you see. She had to get there fast."

"Have you heard from her?"

"She called when she arrived. She is safe, and Vinnie is still alive."

"Well, that's good to hear," Lorna hesitated. "But I really wish one of you had called me. It didn't matter how late it was."

Anya swallowed, "Of course, I understand. But you see, she didn't want to worry you, what with you being so far away."

"Well, I'm not happy about this, Anya. One of you should have called. I'm concerned."

"It happened so fast. I'm sure Miss Doreen will call you today."

"I'm leaving for the airport in about an hour. If you talk to her, please tell her to call me right away."

"I will. Don't worry, Miss. Everything is *just fine* here at the motel."

When Lorna hung up the phone, she had a funny feeling in her gut. Something was not right. She was concerned about Vinnie, but more vexed about why Doreen didn't call her.

Lorna went into her bedroom to pack her suitcase. Her heart beat heavy in her chest.

Something did not feel right.

And she couldn't put her finger on it.

She needed to get home.

TWENTY-ONE
January 6, 1981
Miami Memorial Hospital
Miami

Doreen had fallen into a fitful sleep. She was startled awake by someone tripping over her extended legs.

"'Scuse me." An elderly gentleman mumbled as he shuffled toward an empty chair.

Doreen quickly remembered that she was in the CCU waiting area at Miami Memorial Hospital.

She drew in her legs and sat up straight. She panicked; she needed to call Lorna. "Shit, what time is it?"

"Around ten-thirty." Her cousin Richie, who was sitting across from her, looked like she felt—crusty and achy.

She stood up and looked around for a pay phone. She remembered Vinnie. "Any word?"

"Nah. Still breathing with the tube."

"Where's Eddie?"

"Went to open the station. Betty's on her way. Why don't you head back to the house and get a shower?"

"Yeah, I should do that. But I'm afraid to leave. What if something happens and I'm not here."

Her cousin shrugged. "Gonna happen whether you're here or not. Know what I mean?"

"Yeah, you've got a point there. I'm going to head over to the house. I'll be back as soon as I can. Thanks, Richie." She leaned over him to kiss his cheek.

Richie said, "You know, I like your lady friend. She's real nice. Nice looking, too. Christmas was fun with her. Vinnie liked her, too. We all think you done good, Doe. Real good."

Doreen squeezed his shoulder and left the room.

***

Jacksonville International Airport

Lorna's flight landed on time, and Lindy was at the gate to greet her.

"I really appreciate you taking time out of your day to come and fetch me."

"Oh, any excuse to drive Midnight. It's gorgeous out now, but you know Florida. One minute you're on the beach in full sun, and the next you're running for cover from a deluge! I've got the top down. I hope you don't mind."

"Looking forward to it. I'll give you gas money."

Lindy waved her off. "Not necessary."

They retrieved Lorna's bag. "Do you mind if I make a quick phone call?" Lorna asked.

"How about I bring the car around. I parked in short term. I'll meet you in front."

"Perfect." Lorna made a collect call to the motel. Anya answered and accepted the charges. "Hi. Just landed. Any news from Doreen?"

"Not yet. Is Lindy there now?"

"She's pulling the car around."

"Good. I'm glad you are back safe and sound. Well, I will tell Miss Doreen if she calls that you are on your way back to the motel."

Lorna was about to hang up the phone, but asked, "Anya, is everything else okay? You sound a little weird."

"Weird? What weird? No, everything is just fine. All is well."

Lorna was not convinced.

Something felt so *off*.

***

Pagoda Motel

While Anya was straightening up the lobby for Lorna's arrival, Alice walked in.

"Oh, hello, Miss Alice. So nice to see you today."

"Hi, Anya. Hey, um. Lindy told me she was going to pick Lorna up at the airport because Doreen's uncle had a heart attack?"

"Oh yes, this is true. Miss Doreen is down in Miami right now."

Alice cleared her throat. "Okay, sure. Well, have you heard from Doreen? About her uncle?"

"Oh, si. In the intensive care unit, still with the breathing machines and such."

"Ah, that's too bad. I hope he pulls through. So … um."

Anya stopped dusting. "Yes, Miss?"

Alice fidgeted with things on the reception counter. "Yeah, uh. I was just wondering …"

Anya raised her eyebrows and waited.

Alice blurted out, "Do you know anything about the bones that were found on this property last year?"

Anya took a deep breath and gathered herself into her small strong frame. "*What?*"

Alice ran her hand over her face. "Ah shit."

Anya set down her dust rag and approached her. "Why would you ask?"

"So, it's true?"

"Not so fast. Where did you hear of this?"

Alice swallowed. "I … well, you see. Um. Maybe we'd better sit down."

Anya sat on the edge of the love seat, eyeing Alice. "Go on."

"The other night, Lindy heard something going on in Doreen's cabin. She, ah, actually heard the whole thing."

Anya shook her head and muttered, "Ay caramba."

***

En-route from the airport

Lorna lifted her face to the sun. "Oh man, I really missed this." She called out over the wind that swept through the interior of the car.

Lindy agreed. "I know, isn't this just the bee's knees?"

Lorna closed her eyes and reveled in the air that was Florida. Cleveland was cold and gray with piles of dirty snow shoveled and set back from driveways, walkways, and roads. She couldn't wait to get on the plane. During the flight, Lorna had looked out her window to the land below. The patches of white eventually turned to brown and ecru, the architecture of the Earth gradually sliding into green. By the time she landed, she had felt like she could take in a deep breath and let it out slowly.

Lindy pulled off the highway and into a filling station. "I'm sorry I didn't stop before picking you up. I was running a little late."

Lorna reached for her wallet. "Let me pay."

Lindy waved her off. "Now come on…"

While Lindy held the gas nozzle, she asked, "So, do you want to get some lunch or something? You must be hungry. I know a great little hole-in-the-wall just north of St. Augustine. Their specialty is burgers. Any way you want it, with whatever you want. Their meat is always fresh."

Lorna thought about it for a moment. "Well, okay. But I insist you let me pay since you came all the way up to get me."

Lindy smiled and nodded, "All right, I'll let you do that."

***

Miami

Doreen went into Vinnie's hospital room and sat by the bed. He was trussed up in all kinds of tubes and wires, the breathing machine, along with the IV drip and EKG machine, making whirring noises and clicks.

Doreen watched as his urine bag, attached to a tube that ran underneath the covers, filled slowly with whatever output Vinnie could manage. The man in the bed was becoming a shadow of the man she knew. During the Christmas holiday, she had been keenly aware of his decline as he moved more slowly, his head and neck bent at uncomfortable-looking angles. She was saddened that his once booming voice had gradually lost its timbre. He was dying. And Doreen hoped he would go peacefully in his sleep.

He had once told her he was afraid of dying without dignity, of becoming an invalid for everyone to care for. Betty would chide him. "Oh, you're going to be around for a very long time making us all crazy."

A gentle knock on the door took Doreen out of her thoughts. It was Eddie. He tiptoed in.

"You won't disturb him. He's still out," Doreen quietly said.

"Yeah, I figured." He kissed Doreen lightly on the head. "Nothin' changed, huh?"

"Nope."

Eddie pulled another chair up close with Doreen's and put his hand on Vinnie's leg. "Poor guy."

"Actually, I think he's probably pretty happy right now. Doesn't have to deal with life."

Eddie shrugged. "It's not so bad, really. We got good businesses, money's comin' in, and Richie and me, we take care of everything for him. Betty is always at his side."

"Yeah, but ..." Doreen couldn't explain how she felt about life now. Things were changing for her. Her life at the motel with Lorna, with her new family, the tenants.

Eddie asked, "So, Georgie. What a fuck-up, huh?"

"I don't want to talk about Georgie."

"Vinnie was off the charts mad. I hope it wasn't what caused the heart attack, 'cause if so, I'll go find the little fucker and strangle him with—"

Doreen interrupted. "Ssh., Eddie, leave it be."

Eddie looked sidelong at Doreen. He opened his mouth to continue talking, but Doreen put up her finger. "No."

Pagoda Motel

Anya wrung her hands as she paced the floor of the lobby. "I cannot believe this at all."

Alice watched her pace. "I know. I hope Lindy didn't spill the beans before Doreen has the chance to talk to her."

Anya huffed, "This is not good, not good at all." She looked at Alice, "Did you tell Miss Lindy to maybe not say anything?"

"I did. But she's headstrong, you know what I mean?"

Anya sighed. "This will be very bad for Miss Lorna."

"Why? I mean, it's public knowledge. Well, not the money in the cabin, but the bones."

Anya turned to face Alice. "Miss Alice, what you don't know about Miss Lorna is that she is a very special person, and we protect her first before anything else. When she learned of the bones, it was a very big story. One that Miss Lindy does not understand. And if Miss Lindy tells Miss Lorna about everything, well, it will upset Miss Lorna to no end." Anya did not expound upon how detrimental it could be to Lorna's relationship with Doreen.

Alice stood up, "Well, I think I've done enough damage for one day. I'm going to head back to my cabin and hit the canvas." She hoped Lindy would keep her big mouth shut.

Anya nodded and watched Alice leave the lobby. She did not finish her dusting, but instead went to find Milton to warn him.

***

Diner near St. Augustine

After they ordered, Lindy got right to the point. "So, I was thinking about the new book. I've got several drawings to show you. And I've worked out a bit of a story line." She had brought a small sketch pad, and she opened it for Lorna to see her progress.

Lorna nodded. "Wow! These are amazing, Lindy. You really captured the group. What's your story line?"

"Well, first off, I have a couple of questions about the motel's history."

Lorna sat up a bit straighter. She clasped her hands and waited.

Lindy explained, "See, something happened the other night and I got a bit curious, so I went to the library to research the—"

Lorna's voice was clipped. She leaned in. "What happened the other night, Lindy?"

"Well, it seems as though Doreen has a brother."

Lorna's heart rate increased. She said quietly, "Yes, I know about Doreen's brother."

"Well, you see, the other night I woke up to a lot of raised voices coming from Doreen's cabin. Naturally I went outside to see what was happening. And, well, from what I overheard, apparently there was a lot of money buried underneath the refrigerator, and her brother and his girlfriend came by in the middle of the night to dig—"

Lorna stood up. "Don't say another word. We need to go."

"But what about lunch?"

Lorna collected her purse and started walking toward the cashier desk. "Take it to go. I'll be out in the parking lot. I need to make a phone call." She hastily paid the woman behind the counter and stormed out of the diner.

When the waitress came back to their table with the food, Lindy shrugged and said, "We have to get going. Can you wrap it all up?"

The waitress harrumphed. "Whatever."

Lorna's hand was shaking so badly she could barely slip the quarter into the slot. When she got the operator and her coin clunked down in the return cup, she ignored it.

Anya accepted the charges again.

"What the hell is going on, Anya?"

Anya figured Lindy spilled the beans. "Ah, yes. Well, you see—"

"Anya, I don't have to tell you that this is very upsetting."

"I know, I know. It's all been taken care of, Miss Lorna, and—"

"You need to find Doreen for me. I don't care how many numbers you have to call, but you need to find her for me."

Anya tried to calm her. "Now, Miss Lorna, please try to stay—"

"I'll be home in thirty minutes."

"Ah, yes, Miss."

Anya hung up the handset and scrambled to find the number of the Miami Memorial Hospital.

The nurse at the CCU desk quietly said, "Ma'am, we usually don't do this kind of thing. I can get a message to her, but she will have to call you back on a different phone."

Anya said, "Yes, please have her call me as soon as she can. It is of the utmost importance."

The nurse took the information down and promised Anya she would relay the message when she got off the phone.

Only, the nurse got involved in another, more urgent matter and left the piece of paper near her workstation.

***

Lorna said nothing in the car for the duration of the trip.

Lindy realized she had stepped on a land mine and tried to change the subject, cheer Lorna up a bit, take the pressure off.

"I'm glad you like the sketches. Alice is almost done with the mural on the garage."

Lorna couldn't decide whether she was seething mad or deeply hurt.

Once again, people she trusted were not forthright.

Lorna mumbled to herself as the wind rushed around her head, "And the past just keeps oozing up."

When they pulled into the turnaround at the motel, Lorna got out of the car, pulled her suitcase from the trunk, and said, "Thank you again for coming to get me. Please, feel free to share the food. I'll eat something else later."

Lindy said, "Lorna, I am truly sorry if I said something out of turn."

Lorna looked at her. "I would appreciate you not saying anything to anyone else here. And maybe hold off on your story for a while. I have some things to sort out." She turned and walked into the main building.

The lobby was clean and quiet. The only sound was the rhythmic whir of the ceiling fan.

She took her suitcase upstairs and stripped off her clothes. She needed a shower. She needed to talk to Doreen.

She needed for all this to go away.

TWENTY-TWO
Miami
January 6, 1981

Vincent Anthony Regazzini took his last breath on this Earth at 2:34 p.m.

Doreen was there by his side with Eddie and Betty.

It was Vinnie's wish that he was not to be resuscitated if things went south.

Doreen left the room as the nurses clamored in to pull the tubes and prep him for transport down to the morgue.

She went into the restroom and sobbed. She felt like she was coming unglued. She wasn't ready to lose Vinnie yet. And the incident at the motel weighed heavily on her heart and mind.

Betty came into the restroom and held Doreen, the two women crying on each other's shoulder.

Eddie called Richie and told him to close the station and come up to the hospital. Since Eddie was the eldest, it was his job to alert the attorney and set the paperwork in motion. He also had to make sure the funeral arrangements were in place. Vinnie made him promise that there would be a big party, nothing sad about it! Eddie assured him he would keep that promise.

If there was ever a time Doreen needed her bike, it was now. She wanted the wind to calm her, to whisk the deep sadness away from her—if only for an hour or so.

She remembered something Vinnie liked to say often: "Doe, when all the shit hits the fan at once, it's the trifecta icing on the proverbial 'fuck you' cake, know what I mean?"

Doreen closed her eyes and quietly intoned, "Vinnie, where the hell is that bakery?

TWENTY-THREE
Same day

Every minute that passed without a phone call from Doreen added to Lorna's frustration and concern. She felt like she was being hung out to dry—again.

She would have liked to have known the details from the get-go, would have appreciated better communication from Doreen. She had known something was wrong with Doreen when they'd spoken on Sunday, and this must have been it. And especially in light of the events of the not-so-distant past.

She went over to Doreen's cabin and entered gingerly. It was quiet, smelled a bit like new wood and something vaguely resembling paint or stain.

She went into the kitchen. Everything was where it usually was. She heard the screen door open and turned to see Anya approaching her.

"Hello, Miss Lorna."

"Hi."

"I suppose you have not talked with Miss Doreen yet?"

"You suppose correctly. Have you heard from her?"

"No, Miss, I have not."

The women stood in silence before Lorna said, "You want to tell me what happened here?"

"I think it would be best for Miss Doreen to tell you, really. All I can say is that Milton and I fixed the floor, you can't even tell except that the boards look newer, but it's under the fridge there and—"

Lorna turned to face her. "Anya, I can't go through another time like we did back in June. I just can't."

Anya nodded solemnly but said nothing.

Lorna turned on her heel and left the cabin. She felt as if her world was shriveling.

When Lorna's private phone line lit up fifteen minutes later, she jumped for the receiver.

"Hello?"

"Hi."

"It's about time. Nice of you to finally call. You want to tell me what the hell happened here this past weekend?" Lorna couldn't maintain her cool. She was furious.

"Look, I had no idea about any of this."

"Please, do explain."

Doreen hesitated then said, "There was money buried underneath the floorboards in my cabin—the same cabin that Gino worked out of—and Georgie got wind of it."

"I thought he was in jail?"

"He got released a week ago."

"Let me get this straight. Your grandfather buried money, and Georgie found out about it and made his way up here to dig it up and now ... what?"

"He took the money and ran."

"And how did Georgie find out about it?"

"Vinnie."

"Vinnie ..." Lorna nodded her head as if this made perfect sense. "This story has a lot of holes. Can you *please* fill in the blanks? I don't have to tell you that I'm at my wits' end here! Why didn't you share this on Sunday when we talked? Am I that unapproachable? I had to hear about it from Lindy!"

"Lindy?"

"Yeah, you know, your next-door neighbor; she heard the whole damned thing!"

Doreen hesitated. She was not aware of this. No wonder the shit hit the fan this way. She thought maybe Anya had caved and said something, but now she understood. "Oh, my God. And she told you?"

"That's not the point. All I know is yet another piece of your history has made its way above ground on my property."

Doreen felt her throat constrict. This was not how she had pictured this conversation going. But then again, the last few days were like a twisted horror movie for her. "I ... I

The Ladies of Pagodaville

don't know what to say. I am sorry, Lorna."

Lorna paced. She couldn't hold back her anger. "Well, that's not good enough. What other surprises are in store here, Doreen? Maybe when Vinnie recuperates, you can ask him."

"Yeah. Well, that's not going to happen any time soon, Lorna. Vinnie died a few hours ago." Doreen hung up the phone.

Lorna said, "What? Hello? Doreen?"

Her heart immediately sank. "Oh my God ..." She tossed the handset on the desk and slumped down into her desk chair. "Oh god ..."

Heaving a deep sigh, Lorna put her head in her hands. Even though the situation was maddening, it had unfolded the way it did regardless of how either one of them had intended. She was sure of it. She knew Doreen well enough to know that the family history was a source of pain in her life and she wanted nothing to do with it. But Vinnie was her only link, the man who had raised her into her adult years after her father was gunned down. Now that Vinnie was gone, and with her mother being in Georgia and not active in Doreen's life, Doreen was truly on her own.

Suddenly, Lorna sat up and yanked the Yellow Pages from the desk drawer. She found and dialed the number for Delta Airlines, inquired about the soonest flight to Miami from Jacksonville, and booked herself on it. She had four hours to pull it together and get on a plane.

She was not going to let this slip away from her.

She called Anya, resting the handset between her chin and her shoulder while she gathered some papers. "Hi, can you take me to the airport?"

"You just got home!"

"I'm going to Miami. I have to find Doreen."

"What? Did you speak with her just now?"

"Yes, Vinnie died a few hours ago. We had an argument. I was a heel, and she hung up on me. I've got to find her."

"Yes, we will take you. What time is the flight?"

"In four hours."

"Oh, mi dios, you must hurry."

"I know. Thanks."

Lorna charged up the stairs and threw her clothes on the bed. She jumped into the shower, let the hot water sluice over her body and hair, washed, no *scrubbed*, dried off, pulled her clothes and personal items together again, and repacked her suitcase. She had just enough time to call The House of Vinnie before grabbing something to eat and heading back to Jacksonville.

Betty picked up. "Regazzini household, Betty speakin'."

"Hello, Betty? This is Lorna Hughes."

"Oh! Hello!"

"Hi, listen, I have to make this quick."

"Doreen is resting. Do you want me to wake her?"

"No, actually. You're the person I need to talk to."

"Oh?"

"I'm flying down. My flight gets in at 9:30. I'm going to rent a car. Doreen and I …" She paused. "… had a rather uncomfortable conversation a short while ago and …" She took in a deep breath through her nose and let it out. "I need to make it right."

"Oh? Well, she's very upset about Vinnie, as you can well imagine." Her voice took on a protective tone. "And I don't want to upset her even more."

"I'm understand, but I need to be there for her."

"Well."

"Betty, I am very sorry for your loss. I liked Vinnie. I wish I'd had the chance to get to know him better."

"Well, he liked you too. Gave Doreen his blessing." She sighed. "It's going to be tough going around here for a while."

"I'm sure it is. When my father died last year, it was like a dark dream."

The women were silent for a moment until Lorna said, "Can you give me directions from the airport? Oh, and what is the gate code to get in?"

Betty gave Lorna the necessary information, and Lorna went outside to Anya's waiting van.

TWENTY-FOUR
Same day
Miami

Lorna made her way out of the maze of roads connecting the massive Miami airport north toward Coconut Grove. She followed Betty's directions and found herself at The House of Vinnie forty minutes after leaving the airport.

When she drove through the slowly retracting gates, the motion sensor lights came on and illuminated the entire front walkway, gardens, and door.

The large front doors opened, as if on cue.

Betty waited. "You made it. How was your flight and drive?"

Lorna walked in. "Perfect. The directions were perfect."

"Doreen is still sleeping, believe it or not. She was exhausted from her long drive down here the other night, and she hasn't gotten much sleep since then."

Lorna set her baggage down. "That's good. I'm pretty beat, too. I just got back from Cleveland. It feels like today started three days ago."

Betty nodded. "I can understand that. Well, let me show you to the guest suite."

As Lorna unpacked her bag and situated herself in the room, she thought about running a hot bath in the claw-foot tub located in the massive guest bathroom. There was every amenity one could want: thick plush towels, elegant soaps, candles, a radio and phone built into the wall next to the commode, a bidet, and two deep sinks with a solid wall of mirrors.

The overhead lights were on a dimmer, and she set them low. She turned on the radio and found a jazz station out of Miami. She ran the water hot, poured in some lavender bath bubbles, and stripped down.

Once enveloped in the hot water, she sighed deeply. She couldn't believe she was here, in Miami, having been home for only a few hours. She let her mind wander.

***

Doreen tossed and turned. Her bed sheets were soaked from her sweat. She sat up and wondered where she was.

The darkness confused her.

She put her legs over the side of the bed. It was two o'clock in the morning.

"Shit."

She peeled off her T-shirt and jeans and made her way into the bathroom, the events of the last twenty-four hours slowly coming into view.

The connecting door to the other guest room was slightly open, and she peeked around into the darkened room. When her eyes adjusted, she saw that someone was sleeping in the bed.

She stepped back slowly and quietly closed the door.

She wondered who was in there.

Doreen ran the shower and stood under the pulsing water for at least fifteen minutes.

She felt nauseated and hungry, over-tired and awake at the same time. Her heart sat like a rock in the middle of her chest.

She felt lost.

She knew she should call Lorna back. It was rude to hang up on her. And she did love her. But she would do that later.

Now, she needed some food.

Then she would go back to sleep.

Later that morning, Lorna, Richie, Eddie and Betty were sitting around the breakfast table talking about the funeral party Vinnie insisted on having.

When Doreen came downstairs and into the kitchen, she

did a double take and then froze. She looked at Lorna and mumbled, "When did you get here?"

"Last night. You were sleeping, and I didn't want to disturb you." Lorna added quietly, "Nice to see you, too."

Doreen shook her head, sighed, went to the cabinet, grabbed a coffee mug, and dispensed the coffee. "Why don't we take a little walk?" she said to Lorna.

"Sure." Lorna attempted a small smile for the rest of the family as she rose from the table. "See you later." She said to them.

Doreen led them out a side door and into the gardens that surrounded the property. She turned to look at Lorna. "What are you doing here?"

"Ouch."

"Well, what the hell? A little warning—"

Lorna cut her off. "I'm not very happy with the way we ended our conversation yesterday. Are you?"

Doreen looked away. "No, but I felt like you were coming down on me, and I couldn't breathe."

"I was mad. And for good reason, too."

"You didn't even give me a chance. You just started pumpin' out the bullets."

"Doreen, really? Bullets? Aren't you getting a bit dramatic?"

Doreen sneered. "Not really, Lorna. It sure felt like it."

Lorna shook her head. "I don't understand. How did you think I would feel, coming home to that?"

Doreen shifted gears and raised her voice. "Look, I had no idea that *any* of that family history was still at the motel, okay?"

Lorna started to say something, but Doreen escalated. "You just can't understand that, can you? You know, it's not all about your motel and—"

Lorna interrupted, matching Doreen's raised voice. "Are you saying that your history—and let's not forget about the bones—"

Doreen blew up. "The bones! The fucking bones! How long are you gonna go on about the fucking bones? I didn't do it, Lorna! My bat-shit crazy grandfather did! I came crawling—" Doreen was spitting now, her face beet red. "I came *crawling* back to you to and admitted to *all those people* that I was the granddaughter of a murderer."

Lorna splayed her hands upward. "And now, that murderer's legacy has once again risen from the depths!"

Doreen screamed. "I knew this was a mistake living with you. I knew I wasn't good enough for you, for your dreams, for your way of life! Why the hell did you make me stay?"

Lorna winced at the harsh words and leaned back, away from the heat of Doreen's anger. "Whoa, wait a minute, it was pretty mutual, remember? You wanted to stay as much as—"

Doreen cut her off again. "Sure, you had me help Milton build your garden. What was that? A payoff? Did you think maybe I owed you?"

Lorna felt the walls closing in. She spoke between clenched teeth. "What are you talking about?"

Doreen raised her arms, turned on her heel, and strode off farther into the backyard.

Lorna followed at a trot. "Doreen! Stop!"

Doreen turned and pointed her finger in Lorna's face. "No! You don't get to come down here and keep this shit going. No! You don't get to do that! Maybe the tables are turned now! Maybe it's my turn to tell you to leave! Just go!"

Lorna stopped in her tracks. She looked at the woman in front of her. This woman she fell in love with, this woman who had stolen her heart. Her breath caught in her chest. She put her hands out. "Wait. Calm down. Just take a deep breath."

Doreen turned away from her, sobs wracking her body. "Go away."

Lorna approached her. "No."

Doreen crumpled to the ground on her knees, her chin to her chest.

Lorna kneeled behind her, encircling her with arms.

Doreen wailed.

Betty came running down. When she caught Lorna's eye, Lorna shook her head. Betty stopped, watched for a moment, wrung her hands, then backed away.

Lorna cooed, "It's all right, honey. I've got you."

Doreen tried to talk between her gasps. "I just can't ... I don't know if ... I don't belong ... I feel so lost."

Lorna continued to coo. "I know. I know."

"No, you don't... you have no idea. I feel so ... stained."

Lorna held her tighter. "No, you are *not* stained!"

"I've got this ... beast following me around my whole life. And just when things start to go well ... so well, the monster reaches up and pulls me down again." She hit her fist on her knee.

Lorna hugged her tighter. "C'mon baby. It's all right. There's no beast here."

Doreen continued to shake.

Lorna rode the waves.

When Doreen's sobs finally subsided, Lorna pulled Doreen back toward her so Doreen's back was leaning against her chest. She offered up a crumpled paper napkin. "Here, honey."

"Thanks." She blew her nose and wiped at her eyes. She let her head loll back onto Lorna's shoulder. "Ah God." Her voice was ragged.

Lorna held her. "Talk to me, Doe."

"I wouldn't even know where to start."

Lorna took in a breath and let it out slowly. "How about I apologize for making you feel closed in."

"Accepted."

"And how about I tell you that I am so sorry about Vinnie. I know he was family."

"Thanks. Yeah...he used to drive me crazy, but I loved him anyhow."

They sat in silence. Insects buzzed around them, and birds called to one another from high in the trees. Doreen turned around to face Lorna.

Lorna brushed some loose strands of hair from Doreen's forehead. "You okay?"

Doreen nodded and blew her nose again. She said quietly, "I am so sorry about yelling at you. About the shit that went down at the motel with Georgie. I am so sorry.

Lorna asked, "Honey, why couldn't you tell me about this on Sunday when we talked, when it happened?"

Doreen lowered her head and studied the grass between them. "I panicked."

"Why would you panic?"

"Because ... of ... well, a lot of things."

"Like?"

Doreen looked Lorna in the eye. "Because I didn't want you to think less of me. Things were going along so well."

"Less of you? Why would I think that?"

"My past. My family. The mob. The shame I feel around it."

"Shame?"

"Yeah." Doreen pulled blades of grass up and let them fly away in the gentle breeze. "The beast I was talking about, the one I can't get rid of no matter how many times I try to run from it. It's my heritage."

"Honey, it's not who you are today," Lorna replied. "Your past is where you came from—you had no choice! But your soul and spirit today, that's what counts and that *is* who you are."

Doreen sighed deeply.

"Do you remember a conversation we had several months ago after you decided to stay on at the motel for a while?"

Doreen thought for a moment. "We had a lot of conversations. Refresh my memory."

"You revealed a little bit of yourself to me. You told me how you used to run at the slightest inkling of trouble and how you never stayed in one place long enough to see things through. And that if things were going well, you'd purposefully screw it up."

"Okay. I remember."

"So?"

Doreen shook her head.

Lorna waited.

Doreen said, "Conflict."

"Conflict?"

"I mean, my parents weren't abusive or anything, and we had all the comforts of home. But they didn't know who I was in my heart."

"Who were you?"

"I wanted to be a boy; play ball, ride bicycles, build forts, catch frogs, and help my dad work on the car. I liked to take things apart and try to put them back together again. I was fascinated with the little parts of the bigger things, always good at puzzles, know what I mean?"

"I do. You have amazing talents."

"But I was made to dress up like a little girl, act like a little girl. My mother paraded me around like some little princess. They had this idea about what little girls were supposed to do and act like."

Lorna agreed. "I know the feeling."

Doreen looked off behind Lorna's shoulder, her memories pulling her brows together. "You know, I got sick almost every morning before I had to get on the school bus because I would refuse to dress how she wanted me to dress. I'd be late. And she was embarrassed. In front of all the kids on the bus she'd whup my ass with a fuckin' spatula for sassing her and being late. It was torture. I'd get teased on the bus. Then I'd puke when I got off the bus. It was a vicious cycle."

"Oh, honey."

"I used to dream up these elaborate plans to run away from home. I kept a pencil and paper under the covers at bedtime to draw out the escape routes."

Lorna smiled. "I can picture it now."

"And then ... when I saw my father get gunned down, so much changed. I was fifteen and ready to hate the world. I lived in a fog until we packed up and moved down to Miami, to Vinnie's. When we settled in in Florida, I stuck to myself, went to school, ignored everyone, and learned the trades from my cousins. My mother moved up to Atlanta a year later, and I could finally be who I wanted to be. I practically lived in the garage, barely passed my classes to graduate. I didn't care. All I saw was the open road. I custom built my Harley over the summer, and when I turned eighteen, I hit the open road."

"So, you just traveled?" Lorna added, "A babe in every port?"

"Well, I don't know about the babe part. Sex, yeah, but relationships? Not a one really. Oh, they tried all right. But like I explained to you, I could not find my way into it, so I found my way out and left." She put her head down. "I know I hurt a lot of people. I tried to warn you."

Lorna realized something. She ignored the comment and said quietly, "You know, honey, you and I are a lot alike."

"No way! You're smart, educated, logical. And I'm—"

Lorna cut her off and said matter-of-factly, "While you were busy running from relationships and hardships, I was busy running in place. I hurt a lot of people, too. I compared everyone to Jeanie, and no one measured up. Not a one. And you know what? All the smarts and logic kept me a prisoner. A hostage, *just* like your family status kept you."

Doreen nodded. "Okay."

Lorna continued, "It wasn't until I bought the motel last year that I was finally able to be the person I kept hidden while growing up. Just because you and I have different backgrounds doesn't mean we didn't share the shame and misunderstanding while growing up. I too endured the expectations of being someone my parents thought I *should* be instead of who I *was* in my heart."

"Go on."

"I saw my parent's wealth as a badge that they could use to dictate what I was going to do my life. Key word: *My*!" Lorna narrowed her eyebrows and spoke with rancor. "Be the perfect, well-adjusted daughter. Get consistent high grades, have the right friends, be on all the school committees and teams, date the right boys, go to all the right parties, go my father's alma mater, become a lawyer. So, when *my* dad died, it was as if a locked door flew open and yanked me through!"

"And?"

She lowered her voice and found a gentler tone. "I did. I left the only home I had ever known, the only job I'd had since my mid-twenties, and bought the motel. I put all my eggs into one basket and went for it. There was no other way."

Doreen said, "And then you decided to renovate, and all hell broke loose."

She nodded. "I found myself in a situation that threatened my very core. It scared me because I knew there was no turning back."

"I am so sorry. I should never have come in the first place. Or returned, for that matter."

"But no, you're wrong! What happened was *not* your fault. Fate put us together, don't you see? I would have renovated the tennis court and pool with or without you in the picture. But you being in the picture was supposed to be, don't you get it? Your history, your journey. It was the linchpin to expose the evil and get rid of it." She touched Doreen's cheek. "We're very much alike, you and me."

Doreen nodded slowly.

Lorna leaned in. "I fell for you regardless. I fell for you from the first time I laid eyes on you. You woke up this ... this part of me that I'd buried after Jeanie. I wasn't even sure I had it anymore. You were *supposed* to be there that day in June. We were supposed to make love in the ocean as strangers. I was supposed to send you away, and you were supposed to come back. And, as far as I am concerned, you're supposed to stay."

Doreen kissed Lorna on the mouth. Tenderly and gently. When she pulled back, she murmured, "You think we were put together to help each other heal. Be who we always wanted to be?"

Lorna returned the kiss and took Doreen into a tight embrace. "Yes, I think so." Then she added, "I *know* so."

They sat like that, rocking gently, for what seemed like long minutes. Then they heard the familiar sound of in-ground sprinklers gearing up for a timed spray.

There was one located right between them.

"Oh shit, look out!" Doreen jumped up and grabbed Lorna's hand. They managed to dash away from the onslaught of water before getting completely soaked.

Lorna stopped and pulled Doreen closer to her when they made it to the patio. She said, "We're in this together, Doe.

Right down the line."

Doreen smiled, her deep blue eyes clear and her facial features soft again. "Yeah Lorn, we are. Right. Down. The friggin' line."

TWENTY-FIVE
The Pagoda Motel
January 9, 1981

Lorna and Doreen arrived back at the motel in the late afternoon on Tuesday. They went their separate ways to unpack and get settled. After throwing a load of wash into the wash machine, Lorna settled down to her mail. There was the usual cascade of bills, magazines, and junk mail. There was a letter from Avril she would read later after dinner and the bonfire that usually followed. She separated the bills and put them in a folder for later inspection. She flipped the pages of *The Law Review* without really reading anything specific. She got up, studied her empty cupboards and refrigerator, and decided to head to the grocery store.

While she perused the shelves and filled her carriage with necessities, she thought about a conversation she'd had with Doreen during their long drive north after Vinnie's funeral party.

"What do you think about telling the tenants about the history of the motel?"

"Well, how much do you want to tell? It's a pretty involved story, Lorn," Doreen asked while reaching into a bag of pretzels.

"I know. But I think disclosure is important. I don't like secrets."

"What if we just tell them the basics?" She crunched audibly.

"We could, but ..."

"I mean, how would it change their lives if they know the whole ordeal?"

"I think, actually, it's more for me than for them. I know that sounds selfish."

"Well, yeah, maybe. What about the rest of us? I'm not

terribly proud of what I brought to it. And Anya and those guys played a big part."

"I know." Lorna was having trouble explaining why she felt the way she felt. "What if we talk with the rest of the family before making a decision? Anya told me last year that she was very glad to have everything out in the open. She said it was freeing."

Doreen, who was driving, pulled off the interstate into a rest area. "I'm starving. These pretzels aren't cuttin' it. We might as well gas up." When she turned the engine off, she turned to face Lorna. "Honey, I want you to do what you think is right. If you want to talk to the tenants, I'll be there to support you and add anything that might be helpful. It won't be very comfortable for me, but if I've learned anything on this trip, it's that I have to face parts of my life I've been running from for a long time."

Lorna kissed Doreen on the lips. It was quick but earnest. "I love you."

When Lorna arrived home from her errands and was unpacking her groceries, Anya knocked on the back screen-door. "Hello?"

"Come on in!"

They hugged.

Anya sat down at the table. "I'm glad to see you back. It's been too quiet."

"It's good to be back. How is everything? How are you?"

"Everything is, as you say, copastatic."

"Close enough Would you like something to drink?"

"Sure, maybe some iced tea."

Lorna poured them both a glass and sat down to face her. "I have a few things I'd like to discuss with you."

"Okay."

"How would you feel if I shared the history of the motel with the tenants?"

Anya nodded. "I was wondering when you might want to do this very thing. Maybe it is time, no?"

"I think you're right. Especially with what happened last weekend and how Lindy heard the whole thing."

"Yes."

"It would expose us all."

"Um hm. Yes. But maybe—" Anya took another sip of her tea—"it would be for the best. That way there will be no secrets, or people making up stories."

Lorna played with the condensation on her glass, making circles on the Formica-topped table. "It would clear the air. I got mad at Doreen for what happened. It wasn't her fault, I knew that. But I don't want that between us."

"I understand that, Lorna."

Lorna nodded and looked directly at Anya. A corner of her mouth went up. "Hey, do you know you didn't call me 'Miss'?"

Anya smiled back. "This I know. We decided, while you were gone, that we are family. And we don't call each other with those names in our family."

Lorna felt a warmth in her heart. "I am honored, Anya. Would you like to be in the room when I talk to the tenants?"

Anya thought about it. "No, really, I don't think so. This is best for you to do."

"And I can tell them the whole story, even with Marco?"

"I don't see why not."

Lorna took Anya's hand in hers. "You really are a rock, aren't you?"

"A rock?"

Lorna nodded.

Anya leaned in and winked. "I am more a boulder, no?"

Lorna said quietly, "A mountain."

Lorna felt at that moment that nothing could possibly shake her foundation. Her path was clearly marked. Sharing the history of the motel with her tenants would serve to strengthen the conviction that only love *truly* conquered all.

After Anya left, Lorna organized herself and called a meeting with the tenants.

It was time to let go of the past.

Rain moved the bonfire gathering from the beach to the lobby. Lorna provided drinks.

Lorna started her story from the beginning—how she arrived at the motel, her ideas and plans, and how her eager renovations of the pool and badminton court turned into a gruesome excavation of human remains.

Lorna spoke of her Mexican family with fondness and loyalty, and Doreen interjected her side of the experience when needed.

The group was rapt.

The only question was asked by Lindy. "Did the FBI ever identify the bones?"

Lorna answered, "I wanted nothing to do with it after the FBI released the property back to me. I just wanted them gone. I needed to move on. I can't tell you how horrible it was to think that my new life was going to be shattered by something that had happened so long ago."

PK said, "It took courage, Lorna. That's pretty impressive."

"There was no turning back, ladies. I had to forge forward."

Mari intoned, "And look what you created here. It's so unique."

Lindy agreed. "And all is supposed to be as it is, right?"

Lorna smiled. "Yes. It is." She looked at Doreen. "Well, now that *that* is over with, I have a few other things I'd like to discuss with you. How would you feel if we were to structure this group, us, like a true collective?"

Alice asked, "How do you mean?"

"We make decisions like a group. Everyone gets to have an opinion. For instance, Lindy wants to design a graphic novel about the motel and all of us here. Isn't that right, Lindy?"

Lindy nodded. "Yes. But I didn't want to bring it up again after the recent incident. Now, though, that you're asking us to be active participants in certain decisions, perhaps I can put it out there that this motel, all the history, all of you, would be a wonderful story to share. And I would re-create it within the guidelines we all decide on. Would that work, Lorna?"

Lorna looked at the group, "Well?"

PK shrugged. "Hey, I'm in."

Alice nodded. "Okay."

Mari nodded. "I think it is important to write about what comes from the heart. If I had thought about it first, I might have done the same thing. But Lindy can draw. I cannot." She winked at Lindy.

Doreen replied, "Well, I suppose I should jump on the bandwagon too."

Lorna said. "Okay, if you're going to do this, Lindy, I think all the sketches should be approved by us before you send them on to your publisher. Is everyone okay with that?"

They all nodded.

Lorna continued. "Good! So how about making our Tuesday bonfire the meeting night since others might join us for dinner?"

PK replied, "I've got the studio booked next week Monday through Thursday. We've only got four days to polish two songs."

Lorna asked, "Is Cheenah going to help you?"

"Oh man, you should hear her voice. It's like it was meant to be. She's going to be great, but she's pretty nervous."

"I heard you two singing the other day," Mari said. "It was so beautiful. I was enchanted!"

Lindy said. "I'd like to have some preliminary sketches for us by next Tuesday. PK and Cheenah can decide when they are done at the studio."

Lorna sat back and watched the group come together. It was nice to see them connect. Another notch toward forward motion.

After everyone left, Doreen helped Lorna clean up. "I think that went pretty well, Lorn. Don't you think?"

"I do." She started washing glassware while Doreen dried. "I'm beginning to feel like this is truly a collective."

"Did I mention that I'm meeting with Steve and the sheriff tomorrow to try to get their account for cruiser repairs?"

"No! When did you set that up?"

"When we got back. I called Southern Bell, and they're coming out to install a new phone line for the garage. It's time to get workin'. Steve said he'd talk to the sheriff first."

"I'll bet you'll get their business. And their family's too."

"Are you going to be okay with more people coming around?"

Lorna dried her hands. "Well, I've been thinking about that. How would you feel about putting up a privacy fence around the garage?"

Doreen nodded. "I'm all for that."

"I'll pay for it. And I'll call in some workmen. You don't have to do it."

"Well, actually, I'd like to keep it in the family. Milton's cousin can dig the postholes with his rig. You get the raw materials, and Milton and I will have it up in no time."

Lorna took Doreen by the waist and pulled her closer. "You're sure?"

"I'm sure. I don't think we need to get all kinds of people out here when Milton and I can do the work."

Lorna moved in closer. "You know, you're pretty sexy when you talk construction."

Doreen tossed the towel that was over her shoulder onto the counter and looped her arms around Lorna's waist. "Oh yeah? Whatcha gonna do with all that sexy stuff?"

Lorna moved them toward toward the steps. "I think maybe I should demonstrate. Upstairs. Now."

Doreen picked Lorna up in her arms and carried her up the steps, somewhat clumsily because the stairwell was not very roomy, and into the bedroom. She kicked the door closed with her foot.

Lorna murmured. "God, it's good be home."

***

A quiet knock came from Mari's screen door. When she turned the outside light on, she saw Cheenah smiling through the dark webbing.

"I hope it is not too late?"

Mari opened the door, "No, not at all! I was just sitting down to write my parents a letter. Come in!"

The Ladies of Pagodaville

Cheenah stepped in tentatively. "Well, really. The reason I came by was to see if you wanted to walk down to the beach with me. It stopped raining, and the sky is so very clear right now. So many stars."

Mari smiled. "I would love to. Let me get a sweatshirt."

As they walked down the path to the beach, Mari looked up and breathed deeply. "The air is sultry, not like in New Mexico where sometimes the air so dry it makes you feel like sandpaper sometimes! This sky reminds me of my beloved desert. Have you ever been to the desert, Cheenah?" She kept her eyes skyward.

"No, just the ocean."

"The desert is like the ocean. It goes on as far as the eye can see. If you can imagine it, the mountain range in the very far distance makes a new horizon."

"I can only imagine."

"Well maybe someday you will see the desert."

"That would be nice."

"With me."

Cheenah took in a quick breath. "Well, I think that would be nice, too."

They walked in silence for a moment. "I think you have a beautiful voice," Mari said. "I hear you and PK sing. I believe you will make such wonderful music together."

"Thank you. Yes, I think we will as long as I don't get too nervous in the studio and screw things up!"

Mari playfully elbowed Cheenah, "You're nervous?"

"Oh yes. I know how important this will be for PK and I don't want to …"

"You know, I used to have anxiety when I had to get up to speak in front of many people."

"Do you still have this problem?"

"No, I learned how to breathe right. I used to hold my breath so the words would come out all squeaky like. And then I would feel faint and so sick I would throw up."

"Oh no! In front of the people?"

"No, usually afterward. But I learned how to pace

myself and it really works."

"I'll have to remember that. To breathe."

After a moment, Mari asked somewhat timidly, "So, are you and PK ..."

Cheenah waited. But when Mari didn't say anything else, Cheenah finished the sentence for her. "Together?"

Mari nodded in the dark. "Um hmm."

Cheenah chuckled. "Oh, no. We are not together."

"Oh. Well, do you have a steady? You don't mention anyone. Perhaps it was wrong of me to suggest that you are ..."

"Lesbiana?"

"Well, si."

Cheenah said, "I am."

"Well, that is good to know."

"Oh, and why is that?" Cheenah felt flutters in her chest.

When Mariella did not answer right away, Cheenah added, "Because maybe you know since our Thanksgiving holiday, I have been thinking about you, thinking about your beautiful writing. Remember when you told me that your grandmother inspired you to write the book?"

"I do. I do not tell many people about that history. It is very private, but I felt I could trust you. You are very sincere, Cheenah. I like that about you. You are ... real." She turned to look at her. "And I like real people."

Cheenah took in a deep breath. She was afraid to speak, to lessen the heady, sweet anticipation. It was all vibe now.

Mari broke the silence. "Have you been in many relationships with women?"

"No, just one. And it did not go well. She left me for an Americana."

"I understand."

Cheenah's hand brushed Mari's. Mari took the opportunity to hold it. She weaved her fingers through Cheenah's.

She felt the softness that was Mari's skin. She gently squeezed back. "This is so very nice."

"Yes. It is. I am so glad you stopped by. I was thinking

of you."

"You were?"

Mari pulled them to a stop and turned to face Cheenah. She reached over and stroked Cheenah's face. "You are so lovely."

Cheenah felt her nerves teeter on edge. "As are you."

Mariella ran two fingers down Cheenah's check and around her jaw, then down her neck. "So lovely."

Cheenah shivered.

"Are you cold?"

"No. I'm just …"

Mariella leaned in to kiss Cheenah.

Cheenah held her breath, her eyes wide.

When their lips met, Cheenah was immediately aware of the softness of Mari's mouth. Gentle and kind, no pressure.

Mari pulled back ever so slightly, still so close. She whispered, "Breathe."

TWENTY-SIX
March 10, 1981

Lorna settled in for her phone call with Avril. A glass of wine and a plate of nibbles were at the ready.

She dialed and one of the kids picked up the call. Lorna spoke with him for a moment before hearing the clunk of the receiver dropped on the table while he went to fetch his mother.

Avril came on the line, "Oh, thank God. I can finally have my glass of wine. I just poured it."

"How are you, my friend?"

"I'm hanging in there. We all just got over a nasty cold. The kids gave it to us then we gave it back. The family that sneezes together stays together. The weather has been dreadful. Rainy and cold, gray. I'm thinking of coming down there if things don't improve."

"You don't scare me! When?"

"When I can stay there permanently?" Avril laughed and took a hearty sip of her wine. "So, fill me in on all the fabulousness that is The Pagoda Motel."

"Where to start. First off, guess who is now an item here in Heatherton County?"

"Should I sit down?"

"Mariella and Cheenah."

"What? Oh hallelujah! How long?"

"It's been a few months now. I've never seen Cheenah in a relationship before, never seen this side of her."

"How do you mean?"

"She's like a grown woman. I mean, not that she wasn't before, but now this new love seems to have redefined her.

She cut her hair a while back, and it looks quite stylish. She's even taken to wearing some mascara and lipstick when they go out."

Avril sighed. "Young love …"

"They're not that young! Mariella is forty, and Cheenah is almost thirty-nine."

"Well, maybe more like new love. It's so exciting. I hope the best for them. So, who else, what else?"

"Alice took her portfolio to a gallery in Jacksonville. She's been working on a new series, inspired of course by our beautiful environment, and the curator is very interested in her work. She re-created a smaller rendition of the mural she painted on Doreen's garage, and I have to say it's quite amazing. She has a unique eye. Paints a story within a story. The background could be something plain, like a beach scene, but underneath it she peels layers, and people and things emerge from this whole other dimension. It took me a while to get used to it, but the detail is amazing. You really have to study the painting, even come back to it a few times to find things you might have missed the first time."

Avril was an art history major in college. "The technique is hard to master, but I have a feeling she a natural. From what you've told me, I imagine it's how she sees life. Sometimes genius like that astounds me. I think about my own little world here with Saul and the kids. I can't create art, but I can certainly appreciate its intrinsic value. Is she going to have an opening? A good excuse to come down?"

"If so, I'll let you know."

"So, Doreen. How's everything going?"

"She's busy in the garage. Oh, you will love this. We went up to Jacksonville to check out a few antique stores. She found an old Coke machine, the kind where you open the door and pull out the bottle!"

"Oh, those are cool."

"She bought it for the shop. And it still works and takes quarters! We found a local distributor, and now we have Coke, Orange, Sprite, and Dad's Root Beer delivered weekly. We all use it."

"There is nothing better than an ice-cold Coke from a

thick glass bottle, I say. Unless of course you offer wine first."

"Oh my God, you are such a lush!" Lorna heard the clink of a glass from the other end of the receiver.

"Only recently. So, go on."

"Pfft. So anyhow she was able to get the Heatherton County Police vehicle business. Steve and Jillian bring their personal cars to her, and more people are hearing about her skills. She has also worked on a few motorcycles. She loves it, Av. It's where she flourishes."

"She's come a long way, hasn't she?"

"We both have. Ever since Vinnie's death, our relationship has grown around us. We are a lot alike."

"Really? How so?"

"We both lived two lives. She ran from hers, but it always caught up with her. And I stayed in one place and dug trenches. Do you remember how stuck in neutral I was?"

"I do. You would go from one extreme to the other. When your dad died, it was like the dam broke. It didn't take you long to realize that your future could be something different from what your present was."

"So true. Sometimes, when I look back at where I was a year ago, buying the property sight unseen, going through the inspection, finding Cheenah, Anya, and Milton. It happened so fast. I went with my gut the whole way."

"Yeah, and you're not one to jump into anything. Isn't it funny that I was the cautious one? But, hon, look where you are now. You have overcome some hefty hurdles. I am so proud of you and how in the space of a year you've managed to bring your dream to life."

Lorna nodded to herself. She was proud, too.

"So, tell me more," Avril asked. "What's up with the musician?"

Lorna took a sip of her wine and chased it with a Ritz cracker piled high with ham and cheese. She spoke around the food. "PK and Cheenah did their thing in the studio. Two songs. PK sent the tape to her manager. I guess he's all about the new direction. He thought Cheenah's voice was a good

The Ladies of Pagodaville

match."

"How does Cheenah feel about all of this?"

"After she got over her nerves about singing, I think she's found her creative niche. PK invited me to the studio for the postproduction. It was fascinating. I have never seen so many wires and connectors. And the little soundproof room where Cheenah did her vocal tracks? Very cool. Just like you see in the movies."

"Do you like the songs?"

"Yeah, I do. It's definitely rock and roll but there's a softer, maybe pop-like quality to it. PK wants to start playing live again. She's going to take the demo tape to the clubs around town and in Jacksonville. Wouldn't that be great?"

"I like it, Lorn. The tenants are finding their way. And what about the graphic artist gal, Linda?"

"Lindy. We all saw the preliminary work and agreed that she would change our names and not disclose the location of the motel, only that it was located somewhere warm. Her agent in Chicago thinks it is going to be a hit."

"What's she going to call it?"

"The Ladies of Pagodaville."

"Of course, duh! And Mari? How is her second book coming along?"

"She's tight-lipped about it, and that's okay. She's a night owl. Sometimes I'll see Cheenah leaving Mari's cabin in the early hours of the morning."

Avril added, "And I'll bet she's got a smile on her face. The bird that ate the canary. Walk of shame!"

Lorna chuckled. "You're awful, but yeah, she is very happy."

"Lorn, remember the night you and I had dinner at Fricano's in Little Italy before you started this venture?"

"I do. That was when I told you about the plan and how I wanted to make a little history. You proceeded to tell me I would be making one big-assed mistake. Yep, remember it well!"

"You proved me wrong. So wrong. But you stuck with it—even through the disaster of renovations. You're a true warrior, my friend."

Lorna smiled. "I am truly happy, Avril."

"Truth. You look it, sound it. And you are living it! So, now that you have accomplished this amazing feat, my friend, what is your next adventure?"

Lorna smiled.

-The End-

The Ladies of Pagodaville

About the Author

Ellen Bennett lives in Southwest Michigan on a 20-acre horse farm with her partner of fourteen years, Suzanne J. VanderSalm. They are the loving parents of two rescues Mambo and Dietrich, (currently) eight horses, and the venerable Tigger, a night-stalking crusty, old cat who rules the roost.

Learn more about Ellen at
www.smilingdogpublicationsllc.com

Coming Soon from Ellen Bennett and Smiling Dog Publications, LLC!

Specials message for readers from Ellen Bennett...

The two books published in the Pagodaville series thus far are also available in eBook format...and Audiobooks to be released soon!

    Pagodaville – Book One
    The Ladies of Pagodaville – Book Two

Thank you for your interest in the Pagodaville series.
Is Book Three of the Pagodaville Series forthcoming?
Does the sun rise and set every day?
Does the Pope wear white?
You get the idea…
Stay tuned!

Made in the USA
Monee, IL
01 October 2020